# BFS Horizons #17


**FICTION EDITOR**
Pete Sutton

**ASSISTANT EDITOR**
Nadya Mercik

**POETRY EDITOR**
Ian Hunter

**LAYOUT**
Zena Wilde


the british fantasy society

# About the Cover Artist

Joel Bisaillon, known as Umbra Ludus, is a self-taught freelance digital artist from Montreal. For over 12 years, Joel has been a toiling in the realms of speculative fiction and tabletop role-playing games (TTRPGs), weaving his style into a tapestry of dark, dramatic, and boldly colourful imagery. His creations are a fusion of CGI, digital painting, and a touch of machinima, crafted to evoke emotions and spark the imagination of his audience. His portfolio boasts collaborations with such respected companies as New Comet Games, Lostlorn Games, and Legendary Games. Moreover, his work has graced the pages of publications including *Aurealis Science Fiction & Fantasy Magazine, Leading Edge, Electric Spec E-Zine, Hyphenpunk,* and most recently, the cover of *BFS Horizons.*
Portfolio: https://www.artstation.com/umbraludus
All else: https://linktr.ee/umbraludusproductions

First published in the UK in 2024 by

# The British Fantasy Society

www.britishfantasysociety.co.uk

BFS Horizons © 2024 The British Fantasy Society

ISBN 978-1-916652-04-0
Cover illustration © Jenni Coutts
All contributions © their respective authors / artists

# Contents


**8**  **Fell**
Sadie Maskery

**9**  **The Last Shore**
Matthew Owen Jones

**18**  **That Where Sleep Dies**
Maxwell I. Gold

**19**  **What Might Have Been Yet Never Was**
Marge Simon

**20**  **When My Dog Was the Universe**
Katie McIvor

**24**  **Fenrir**
Phil Emery

**25**  **What I Know About the Visitor From Two Nights Ago**
Emma Mary Currans

**37**  **Dietary Advice**
P.S. Cottier

**38**  **Watching the Stars**
Gustavo Bondoni

**44**  **Till Next Time**
A.N. Myers

**53**  **An Informational Plaque Outside the Cathedral of St. Onesiphorus**
Naomi Libicki

**54**    **Slow, Slow, Quick Quick Slow A Six-Hand Reel to the Music of Time**
Marion Pitman

**56**    **The Emperor's Funeral**
Jon Hansen

**58**    **Shadows & Dust**
G.O. Clark

**60**    **The True Ballad of Sir Elinore**
Jess Hyslop

**67**    **Order of Service**
Joe Durham

**72**    **Spacism**
Debasish Mishra

**74**    **The Coming of the Djinn**
Christine Butterworth-McDermott

**76**    **The Camera Trapper**
Alice Hughes

**85**    **A Rock and a Light**
Anna Ziegelhof

**96**    **The Scholar's Claim**
Michael Vance

**113**    **Birds of a Feather**
Sarina Dorie

**122**    **When the White Peak of Nuraghad Calls Them Home**
Keira Reynolds

| | |
|---|---|
| **128** | **Rara Avis**<br>Bruce Boston |
| **130** | **Alice on Shrooms**<br>Allen Ashley |
| **132** | **Lighthouse**<br>Robin Maginn |
| **139** | **Stitches**<br>David Calbert |
| **148** | **Licked Clean**<br>Jen Cornick |
| **155** | **Soliloquy of an Inverted Solipsist**<br>Taliesin Gore |
| **156** | **Contact the BFS** |

# Editorial

I seem to remember writing the Issue 15 editorial with a wish to forget 2022. Well 2023 continued in the same vein, life continues to be demanding and I can only apologise to those of you who didn't get issues 15 & 16 until 2024. We swapped to IngramSpark for our printing because this allowed us to also publish and sell copies on e.g. Amazon (who I hear a big deal in the book selling world?) but that has come with some... challenges. At one point over the Christmas period I was literally begging IngramSpark to take my money as they'd blocked my IP address due to me using their ordering system too much (each member was an individual order) – hopefully this won't be an issue in the future and it's possible that the delay to #17 (due to the delays to #15 & #16) will be the last delay – and that this year (although the winter edition comes at the beginning rather than the end of the year) will mean that there will, be a Spring and a second winter edition. Watch this space I guess.

I'd like to welcome Jenni Coutts to the team as Art Editor with thanks for the cover of this issue, thanks also to Ian Hunter for his poet wrangling skills, thanks to Nadya Mercick for her support as Assistant Editor and thanks to slush readers past and present for this issue – Beth, Lauren, Neil, Robin, Veronika and Alan

Pete Sutton, March 2024

# Fell

by Sadie Maskery

We were made but new born, unbroken,
and when the towers tumbled so did we,
out of the tales. No history tells the truth
completely, evil came from both sides
but so too a little goodness, just a little.
The book is closed, morals drawn neatly
as bedsheets. Lights are quenched
and we are beyond your reach now,
cries echoing in your children's dreams.
Beauty does not define worth, or right,
but yes, we are beautiful in our own way,
sinews and fiery strength, the ripple of
wings skirling and free above the stars.

Sadie Maskery lives in Scotland by the sea. Her latest chapbook, *Love Shanty*, is published by Mariscat Press, and some of her artwork is available from Red Ogre at https://ogre.red/issues/art/art-prints-maskery-sadie

# The Last Shore

## by Matthew Owen Jones

The solitary figure of the old man shuffled along the shore, occasionally stooping to examine some fresh curiosity that had washed up upon the tide. As he moved further along the shoreline, he lurched under the weight of the net slung across one shoulder containing his morning's findings. Each was unique, with a value that he could never know. Layered upon his once broad shoulders were the many necklaces of shells that clattered in the breeze.

The old man paused as he noticed something glittering in the sunlight, and grunted as he bent to retrieve it. It was a golden locket that was wedged beneath a rock. Frowning he tugged it free, wondering how many times he had passed by the object, as it lay at the mercy of the tides.

He washed the sand from its surface in a nearby rock pool and examined its condition. His expression soured further as he saw the barnacles that had begun to grow along one edge, the surface had fared no better and was worn with scratches from exposure to the waves. He was getting older, and his eyes were not as sharp as they once were, but still, such mistakes were unforgivable. Each object washed up here for a reason, and it was his entrusted responsibility to care for them.

He knew the old caretaker would have harshly disciplined him for such negligence. That same irritable old man that had raised him, had also instilled in him a sense of pride in his work and opened his eyes to the great responsibility that they had inherited. A responsibility that was now his alone. Even now, so many years later, he missed that old man. Without him, it was a quiet and lonely existence. Lately, he had grown weary, the bleakness of his routine wore upon his soul.

Sighing, he placed the locket carefully among the other objects he had found that morning and continued his patrol. The old man knew he had little time left before the tide turned and began its retreat, taking its precious secrets with it, some perhaps never to return.

He ambled further along the beach toward the rocky cove, in the shelter of the headland. Since he was a child, it had always been his favourite part of the shore, here the sand and pebbles were replaced by a countless number of shells worn smooth by sea, each a beautiful curiosity, with its own tale to tell. The tall granite cliffs of the cove's dark stone contrasted pleasingly with the carpet of white shells that layered the ground.

The currents that he knew so well would rarely wash any new prize into the cove, but it had been known to happen. He prided himself on his thoroughness and he would search the cove, as he always did at the end of each morning, even if it were a fruitless task.

Toward noon the waves often calmed, allowing him to hear the crunch of shells beneath his crude sandals. It was a peaceful place to come and be alone with his thoughts.

He had almost reached the end of the shore when he saw the wooden box floating in a small channel, flooded by the tide. The old man gently set aside his net of findings and waded into the saltwater among the long green strands of seaweed. The box was rounded like a cask and was the size of a man's torso. He carefully dragged the heavy cask onto the surface of shells and sand. It was carved from a light wood, the intricate detail on its surface showed the quality of its workmanship.

He knew at once that it was special. So large a find, in such an unusual place. He brushed his hands respectfully over its surface, his fingers encountering a metal clasp that held the lid in place. His old hands slid the clasp smoothly to one side, and slowly he lifted the lid. Swaddled in a delicate blue cloth was the pale form of a newborn child. The child flinched in the harsh light of day, shying away in  discomfort. The old man closed the lid in shock. Never had he encountered such a strange thing.

Slowly he opened the lid again as if to confirm what his eyes had seen, the child made soft little noises and shifted weakly at his disturbance. He touched it cautiously with a finger, as it stared back at him with wide blue eyes. The child's flesh was soft and pale, in contrast to the deep bronze of his own weathered skin.

Always before it had been treasures and precious curiosities, never had he seen the ocean bring him a living thing. But the Shore did not make mistakes. Carrying the heavy cask awkwardly in his arms, the old man lumbered back across the sand, toward the cave that served as his home.

His cave was a long hollow scar in the great cliff, with soft, worn pebbles for the floor. It had long served his purpose, and that of the caretaker before him. He gently lifted the child onto the smooth slab of rock that he used for a table, still swaddled in its large blue cloth. The child's eyes were closed as it slept. He stood over it, hesitating, before turning away to complete his daily tasks. The treasures needed his attention. He took a flaming branch from the fire to light his way and, holding the net of his findings clenched in his other hand, he walked toward the back of the cave.

The cavern cut deep into the rock, like a great jagged wound in the earth.

He only came here to place the treasures; it would not be respectful to do otherwise. The narrow passage beyond his cave wound down into the thickening dark, beyond the light of day.

The flickering light of his torch illuminated the old rocks, marked with symbols and inscriptions, that had faded with time. This deep below the surface, the air felt heavy and stale in keeping with the solemn nature of the place. As the passageway opened, he never failed to feel the humbling grandeur of the chamber before him.

The vast cavern stretched before him into the dark. Great stalactites reached from the roof of the cavern far above, like the fingers of a giant, frozen in time.

The old man shuffled forward seeking the alcoves that he would need. As he walked his torchlight spilt upon the dusty treasures of the past, wondrous ornaments and trinkets of silver, gold and exotic woods, each set in a small alcove or upon a shelf of rock.

He felt unworthy to be among so many lifetimes of accumulated treasures, it was his privilege to walk among them. He had been told by the one who raised him that eventually at the end of time, all things would return here.

He knew there would be a resting place specifically chosen for each treasure. The old man wandered in the gloom until he found the one that felt right for each. Lastly, he found the place the locket belonged, upon a small hollow high in the rock. After placing it reverently, he stepped back and grunted in satisfaction. Casting a last look back into the darkness, he began his ascent.

As the seasons passed, the old man continued in his unfailing daily ritual. He would scour the beach carrying the child secured in a sling wrap at his chest, and on colder days he would wear his ragged blue cloak, to shelter them as much as it allowed.

In time the boy grew useful, and as the old man aged, he would watch smiling as he plunged into the sea to retrieve some treasure that floated upon the breaking waves.

At first, it had seemed an intrusion and a burden to care for a child, along with his other responsibilities. But as the years passed, he grew used to the company, and the new presence at his side brightened his world. The old man found it pleasing to pass on his lifetime of accumulated wisdom. The once lonely evenings became more bearable as he found companionship again, after so many years.

The boy played quietly in the rock pool of the cave, examining a crab that had wandered from the rocks, as the old man gazed out toward the ocean and its waves. He wondered how far each wave travelled, before it returned here once more. Like a living thing, the breath of the ocean waves rose and fell upon the shore, with a rhythm that had been there all his life.

"Blue?" The previous year the boy had asked the old man's name, and he had remembered the old caretaker used to sometimes call him Blue, because of his pale blue eyes. He had liked hearing the old name again from the boy's lips.

"Yes?" The old man paused in his preparation of boiling limpets for their supper, looking across at the boy who had shared his cave these last twelve years.

"What is beyond the headland?" Blue met the boy's gaze, wondering at his endless curiosity. He vaguely remembered he, too, had similar questions when he was young.

"*Nothing* lies beyond the headlands. They are impassable, the Shore is the world." He smiled reassuringly as he spoke, repeating the old familiar words that were once told to him.

"The Shore provides everything we need, and always will."

Something within the boy's posture told him that his answer was not enough. The boy stared down into the waters of the rock pool making ripples with his feet.

"Where do the treasures come from?"

Blue looked back out from the cave mouth, toward waves that crashed faintly upon the shore, as though he could read its secrets by looking hard enough.

"Some things are not for us to know. When the tides bring them to us, it is because they have served their purpose, and their time has passed."

"We are merely the caretakers." He added, not knowing what more he could say.

He knew the boy must learn to commit himself to their task and forget such idle curiosities. There was much for him to learn in the subtleties of the tides and their currents, that ever shifted with the seasons. The sea needed to be watched each morning, to predict the likely undercurrents when objects might be trapped beneath the surface, or soon drawn back beneath the waves. It took years of experience to understand its ebb and flow, to share in the secrets it held.

The old man picked at the boiled limpets and seaweed, chewing with old, blunt teeth as he considered the work that tomorrow would bring. The spring tides were due in the next few days, and the harvest would often be heavier during such times. The ocean would come in further, flooding much of the shore.

During spring tides, the treasures could sometimes become caught on the rocks and weeds by the Stack. The Stack was a tall column of black rock that became partially submerged, during the highest of tides. A feature of the Shore that had caused him trouble in the past.

It could be dangerous to reach the Stack in such tides, the Undertow current that formed there was easily strong enough to drag a man, or child beneath the waves and hold him there until he drowned. He resolved himself to move the boy's lessons to more mature matters.

"Tonight I shall teach you about the Undertow. You are old enough now to know such things." Blue's leathery face carried the weight of his years, as he spoke of the Shore's darker nature.

The boy stopped his playing and came to sit at the old man's feet, listening attentively.

"It is a dangerous and unpredictable thing. The Undertow is the current that runs beneath the tide and entrusts the treasures to us. It brings us what it wills... and reclaims that which does not belong." He could see the confusion in the boy's face, as he digested his words. The old man nodded his confirmation.

"Not everything is worthy of a place here, some things are only passing through. The tide returns them from where they came." Blue leant in closer to the boy, to better judge his understanding.

"Just sometimes, a strange tide will bring a bone upon the shore. It is forbidden to take them. If you see one, you leave it be. Do you understand me?" The boy nodded wide-eyed at the revelation.

"*The Undertow takes what does not belong.*" The old man emphasised the seriousness of his words.


Blue awoke early, fastening his ragged cloak as he stepped out into the winds that whipped about him in the fresh morning breeze. Already the tide was beginning to roll in upon the crashing waves, showing some measure of its building strength.

He leant upon the staff that now supported his ageing legs as he stared out into the ocean, reading the currents in the rise and fall of the waves in the sunlight.

Above him the gulls banked and dived upon the winds, they knew of the swells and the bounty it would bring. He watched them, remembering the old caretaker's words – *The sea whispers its secrets, to those who pause to listen.*

The arrival of the boy jolted him from his thoughts. Dragging his gaze from the ocean, he looked upon the boy, and saw the man he was quickly becoming. His shoulders had broadened, and his skin was becoming toned and darker from his days working the shore. Today his young strength would be welcome.

The boy wore the fine cloth he was swaddled in as a babe as a cloak, the colour well suited his eyes that were the colour of the ocean. The old man clasped him on the shoulder.

"Come, we should hurry to beat the tide."

The two of them began by searching the near headland, the old man working the shore, while the boy waded in the shallows, both intent upon their task.

As the day drew on the swell grew, and the waves crashed upon the rocks, scattering plumes of white spray upon the breeze.

A large tangle of seaweed and algae had covered the rolling surface, brought in by the surging spring tide. The thick green weed made searching the ever-shifting shallows slow and difficult.

As the morning turned toward noon, they had made less progress than the old man had hoped. Both he and the boy had found small curiosities – a necklace of coloured glass beads set in gold, and a beautiful carving of a mouse in polished red wood, that made the boy laugh in delight at the discovery.

Despite the precious finds, they had not yet finished scouring the length of the shore. Weary and drenched from the sea spray, the old man beckoned them on toward the cove. The waves had grown in intensity, as the sea had swollen with the high tide. The two of them waded into the waters of the cove, the old man using his staff to steady himself against the current. Here in the cove with a rustling whisper, the sea dragged the shells out before dashing them against the shore in a thunderous crash of surf and foam.

Above the boom of the waves, he heard the boy shout and saw him motion that he had seen something, out toward the Stack. Blue squinted, shading his eyes against the sun with his hand. Soon he glimpsed a shape bobbing upon the waves where the boy had pointed.

The old man nodded his agreement, and the two of them waded further out into the surging waters. He was breathing hard by the time he passed the breakers, and felt relief as chest-deep in the water the waves became less intense.

The boy had plunged ahead, quickly reaching the looming stone of the Stack. The old man saw him clamber onto its slippery surface as a vantage point, to locate the treasure he had seen. Blue, now shoulder-deep in the heaving water, reached the Stack and steadied himself against its reassuring surface. He could feel the tug of the stronger current here, pulling at his legs.

He saw the boy dive below the surface lost from sight, as the old man strained for a glimpse of him. Long tense moments passed before he resurfaced, holding aloft an ornate bird cage carved from wood. The old man smiled at the boy's tenacity, as he watched him wading back through the waves, carrying his prize aloft above the heaving water.

Blue was about to turn and follow when he noticed some dark material beneath the water at the base of the rock. It seemed snagged on some tangle. The old man reached his arm down toward the material, touching it with his fingertips, just barely beyond his grasp. He plunged his arm beneath the water, catching it in his fist, and began to haul it up to the surface. He could feel the resistance weighing it down and suspected it must have become tangled in the long kelp bed that grew here around the Stack. As it rose to the surface, he saw it was a blue rag snagged around something heavy. With a final effort he tugged it free of the water, and with sudden horror realised it was entangled within the remains of a man's rib cage.

He felt cold with the growing realisation he had broken the taboo, by disturbing the bones. Blue shook his head as he stared down at the contents of his hands as though he could deny what he saw.

The look of horror was reflected in the expression of the boy, as their gazes met across the waves. Trembling, the old man released his grip, and let his discovery sink back under the surface.

In shock, Blue began stumbling back through the waves toward the shore as his foot caught among the dense kelp beneath the water. He tugged at it forcefully as the tide surged around him. Off balance the old man slipped and fell, plunging into the cold saltwater that smothered his senses. He struggled to regain his feet, thrashing frantically against the powerful tug of the current that drew him under.

He knew at once that he was caught in the powerful Undertow. It swept him helplessly further from the shore, twisting him down from the fading light of the surface. Blue reached upward toward the receding light, as the last of his air trickled through his lips.

The Undertow embraced him, dragging him deeper into a great trench that he knew would become his grave. His body spasmed as seawater finally entered his lungs, and he floated listlessly downward.

In the gloom of the faint light, as his vision blurred, he could see the hundreds of skeletons scattered around him, entwined among the seaweed and twists of rotting blue cloth.

The boy watched as the old man was snatched beneath the water. He knew Blue would not resurface.

He had never been alone before, and he felt the weight of his sudden sadness. In the last few years, the old man had grown slow, and weak as his eyesight failed. The boy had known he was no longer worthy of the Shore, but did not have the heart to tell him.

He knew the Undertow took what did not belong, and the tide did not make mistakes.

Matthew Owen Jones is an English author, currently living in Canada. He enjoys writing of lonely characters in vibrant worlds.

# That Where Sleep Dies

by Maxwell I. Gold

I am all that is, and ever was
the endless kiss to embrace and consume
that which never sleeps and lay inside deep cellars,
the comfort of stars and children
who'll cry no more,
but laugh under my endless kiss,
where sleep dies

Cradled forever in brittle arms,
Too late before my final touch,
Pulled them closer towards
That which never sleeps, inside my deep, dark cellars,
The nightmares of stars and children
who'll cry no more,
and watch the last moments of history
where sleep dies
for I am all that is, and ever was,

I am Someday.

Maxwell I. Gold is a Jewish American multiple award nominated author who writes prose poetry and short stories in cosmic horror and weird fiction with half a decade of writing experience. Five-time Rhysling Award nominee, and two-time Pushcart Award nominee, find him at www. thewellsoftheweird.com.

# What Might Have Been Yet Never Was

## by Marge Simon

A distant tower, a woman in a white dress parts the curtains to the sea:
a magician's hologram, with seagulls stitched to the waves, the edges of
the horizon.
On the beach a coffin, its nails undone by the tide, fair passage for the salt-
silt soul of he who dares.

His eyes are black, hidden within rings of tattoos. He sees her reflection
in sea glass, knows her from shell-whispers. His legs are mountains, his
arms sequoias; histories are buried in the lines of his face. His signals
ripple the sky.

Their eyes meet & linger, only a finger apart. She evades his eyes, lights
candles with her lips. With a sigh, she draws the curtains whisper-rustle
shut.

Marge Simon lives in Ocala, FL, City of Trees with her husband, poet/
writer Bruce Boston and the ghosts of two cats.  She edits a column for the
*HWA Newsletter, Blood & Spades: Poets of the Dark Side.* Marge's works
have appeared in *Pedestal Magazine, Asimov's, The Magazine of F&SF,
New Myths, Daily Science Fiction.* She attends the ICFA annually as a
guest poet/writer and is a founding member of the Speculative Literary
Foundation. A multiple Bram Stoker award winner, Marge is the second
woman to be acknowledged by the SF &F Poetry Association with a Grand
Master Award. She received the HWA Lifetime Achievement award in
2021. Website: http://www.margesimon.com

# When My Dog Was the Universe

by Katie McIvor

**B**yron was being a good boy. As we sailed over the grasslands, his flopped-back ears and dangling tongue drew smiles from all around the waiting room. He lazed at my feet, blinking. A million stars glowed from the tips of his fur.

The elderly person ahead of me in the queue asked, "May I pet him?"

"Sure."

The person's central eye scrunched up. They extended a lightly feathered appendage. Byron nudged his head up, panting with delight.

"Oh," said the elderly person. "He's frazzly!"

"It's the static," I said, embarrassed. I had grown used to the way the energy of the universe sparked through Byron's fur, turning his ears to velvet crackle tubes. The miniscule shocks kept me awake at night, but then I was awake anyway.

"He's lovely," the person said.

They sounded wistful. I wanted to ask why, to ask what they were doing there, but I didn't, because I didn't want to be asked in return. Nobody comes to the End of the World without good reason.

The waiting room drifted along the tracks like a wonderland safari. The whole complex was built on rails which circled the planet, leaving the ground below an untouched paradise for the numerous rare species of the Plains. Occasionally a bird soared past the windows and Byron froze, head lifted, tongue suspended. *Toba would love it here,* I thought. A familiar cold weight slipped down my throat and deep into my stomach.

The elderly person was called.

I started to feel nervous. I sat on the floor with Byron. He licked my

face, the static setting my hair on end. The inside of his mouth was an exploding nebula of colours.

At last, the Endguard called my name. We walked along a cylindrical, grass-walled tunnel to her office. Byron cocked his leg and I started to apologise, but the Endguard laughed. "Good for the grass," she said.

Tiny flowers erupted, bloomed, and evaporated into swift puffs of pollen where Byron had peed.

"So," said the Endguard, settling herself into a curved chair in her office. "I think I can already see what the problem is."

"It was my fault," I said, and then I couldn't go on. I looked down at Byron's soft, glittering head. I had dragged him here, through the depths of space, across universes, to the ends of everything. I had done this to him. And yet he smiled up at me, as placid and trusting as ever.

"Why don't we start at the beginning?" The Endguard plonked a box of tissues down on the desk.

I took a deep breath and told her everything. How happy we had been, just me and Toba and Byron. We weren't well-off, but we had everything we needed. I described the field behind our house, where Toba foraged for broadleaf plantain, and the wood where we walked Byron. Our home seemed as clear in my mind as if I had been there only yesterday, though in reality, we had been travelling for many months since Toba died.

My voice broke at this point. I reached for the tissues.

"An accident?" asked the Endguard gently.

"An illness," I choked. "It was over very fast."

"That's a mercy," murmured the Endguard. "And then what happened?"

"I don't know," I said. I closed my eyes, trying to picture what I'd seen, what I'd done. "The room just... folded up. I was holding Toba's hand. Then she was gone, and everything got smaller and smaller and spiralled in towards me. I didn't know what to do. So I reached out for the nearest thing I could find, which was... "

"Your dog," finished the Endguard.

I nodded. My throat felt filled with tar.

"Don't worry," the Endguard said. "We see this kind of thing a lot, you know. More than you'd think."

*But how*, I wanted to ask. *How is any of this possible?* Instead, I asked, "Can you fix it?"

"You mean, restore the universe?" said the Endguard. "Usually, yes. It's not an easy process – grief is an incredibly powerful force, after all – but we'll give it a go. The question is, though, what would *you* like to do now?"

I shrugged.

"Come on," said the Endguard. "There must be something you want. Or someone?"

She looked at me, a meaningful tilt to her head.

"I just want Toba back," I said.

"Perfect!" she replied, as though I had requested nothing more onerous than a cup of coffee. "Well, all the data we need is right here inside this good boy" —Byron thumped his tail— "so we'll get started. Why don't you wait outside, in the park? I'll send him out to you."

I nodded. My heart was knocking in a crazed, desperate rhythm. Was it possible to go insane with hope?

Outside, the twin suns had set. A haze of stars hung above the park at the rear of the complex. Over the safety railing, I could see the endless grasslands below, where wild animals stirred and twitched in their sleep.

I closed my eyes. The loss, the horror, the months of travel, of trying to put things right – the whole time asking myself *how?* and *why?* and *why me?* – it all crashed over me in a wave so overpowering I thought I would drown. I knelt, pressing my hands into my eyes. They were busy taking the universe out of my dog, so I couldn't even hold him.

At last, my tears subsided. I sat in the soft grass, hiccoughing, my mind empty. The night air whispered across my face.

The door to the complex opened, and Byron bounded out. His fur was a matt chocolate-brown, no longer sparkling with uncountable stars. He gambolled across the park like a puppy.

With him was a small, beloved figure whom I recognised as a piece of my own heart.

It was time to stop questioning. I got up and walked towards my family.

Katie McIvor is a writer from the Scottish Borders. She studied at the University of Cambridge and now lives in the Borders with her husband and newborn baby daughter. When not changing nappies in the middle of the night, she enjoys going for long walks with her two dogs. Her short fiction can be found in magazines including *The Deadlands, Interzone, Fusion Fragment,* and *Little Blue Marble,* as well as the Bram Stoker Award-nominated anthology *Mother: Tales of Love and Terror* (Weird Little Worlds Press). Her three-story mini-collection in support of the Scottish Wildlife Trust is out now with Ram Eye Press. Find her on Twitter @_McKatie_ or on her website: katiemcivor.com.

# Fenrir

by Phil Emery

The wolf knows the way  
Moving through hackles of myth  
sheltering cubs from the bad  
press meted out in fantasy novels  
stealthily threading wildwoods of unease  
padding through folklores of snow and spruce  
in packs of fears or  
aloned  
in calls of twilight  
Each wolf is the last  
as the light fades from the world's eyes  
Every wolf is the last wolf in the heart of its gaze  
Shadowing the path that has always been  
over cambered gotterdammerunged dusks  
across endless escritoires of evening  
Always knowing the way  

Phil Emery has been published in the UK, USA, Europe and Canada since the seventies. His novel, *Necromantra*, was published in 2005 by Immanion Press, and reissued in a revised second edition in 2015. His various stories have been published in US and UK fantasy anthologies and another novel-length fantasy, *The Shadow Cycles* was published in 2011. Besides two collections of short stories and verse, *The Celt in the Machine* and *Arabesques from the Edge of Time,* and a collection of gothic monologues; latest publications include the S&S tales "Seven Thrones," "Demonic," and "Threnody of Ghosts" in the recent Swords & Sorceries Parallel Universe anthologies. Another S&S piece will be included in the forthcoming Rogue Blades anthology *Neither Beg nor Yield,* and the absurdist cyberpunk graphic novel with artist Toeken, *Razor's Edge,* is due out from Android Press later this year.

# What I Know About the Visitor From Two Nights Ago

by Emma Mary Currans

I will tell you all I can, but I won't tell you for free. There's a hole in the chapel roof that needs fixing, and we haven't the funds. The Council of Saints are as stingy as ever, especially when it comes to back-of-beyond convents like ours.

Do we have a deal? Good. Then I suppose I should start with the blizzard.

People often seek shelter here when the weather turns bad. Most of the time, it's students from the Tower who've taken lodgings in the village, having staggered out of the pub in the early hours, too intoxicated to find their way home. Grandmother lets them sleep in the kitchen, by the fire – she'll not have ghost-talkers in the dormitories, you see. Not half-trained ones, and *especially* not drunk half-trained ones. She says they're liable to cause a disturbance.

So, we're used to ushering people in from the storm in the middle of the night. I daresay if they'd just shown up hammering on the door and yelling, someone would've shown them to the kitchen, and they'd have been gone by morning. But it wasn't shouting that woke us, no. It was the bells.

Now, the bells – they don't normally sound of their own accord. Generally speaking, they chime when someone pulls on the rope. And if no one's on the rope, it means the wards have been tripped.

There's a fence around our lands, and it's not made of wood or wire. It doesn't keep anything out, but it does warn us when something nasty's heading up the path. Creatures from Up the Hill. Displaced spirits that never found their way to Hell. Representatives from the Council.

If the bells are singing of their own volition, whatever's at the door isn't something you want to let in.

Naturally, we brought the works. Oh, you wouldn't think it to see us on a normal day, tending the gardens or copying out manuscripts, but we make for a formidable sight when we're threatened. We gathered in the entrance hall, the Mothers with their crossbows, the Aunts with their spools of golden thread, ten of the eldest Sisters forming a line at the back. I was among the other Mothers, a bolt trained on the thick oak doors and – I'm not so proud that I'd deny it –scared witless. I've seen things come through those doors that were taken down with a single shot or bound and banished with the merest wisp of thread. But I've also seen things that would give you the kind of nightmares that leave you afraid of your bed.

Have you noticed that the woman we call Grandmother is rather young for the title? She should be a Mother yet. But her predecessor, who was still cultivating her for the role, answered the door on a night much like that of the blizzard. She was lost along with two Mothers and an Aunt, but you'll not find them in the graveyard. There wasn't enough to bury.

I was trying not to remember this when our current Grandmother and Great Aunt swept through the crowd, and we parted for them like water. You may not understand this, being from the safe bubble of the city, but when danger comes calling, we always answer. Otherwise, it'll hang around, and – well, have you heard of the convent over at Candle Rise?

No. Of course, you haven't.

*That's* what happens if you don't deal with the problem while it's on your doorstep. Because while it's on the doorstep, you know where it is and what it's doing. Heaven help you if you let it out of your sight.

I remember how Grandmother and Great Aunt looked at each other. How they said the shortest prayer in the canon, to the Watching Angel. Then they each took one of the great iron handles and wrenched the doors open.

What we saw in the snow looked like a girl, but on such a night, with the bells still screaming, that meant very little.

Someone fired. Not me, I hasten to add. That was one of the armed Sisters, a girl on the Mother path, a jittery young thing who'd never been called to defend the convent before. The bolt struck the doorframe and sank into the wood, soft and warped by the weather, and she might have set off a whole wave of panicked fire had Great Aunt not raised a glowing tangle of thread.

Stillness washed over us, our limbs locking in place. Oh, she only uses such power when she has to, I understand that, but until it happens to you, you cannot know the terror of it. To feel your mind thrash and cry out while your body stands so serenely, unable to voice your screams... it is, I think, much like the moment of one's own death.

Grandmother and Great Aunt approached the figure in the snow and Grandmother turned her over. From where I stood, she seemed human enough, though I thought she might be dead. She made a pretty corpse, you know. She'd been looked after very well in life, but it was plain to me that she was not loved. Her clothes were fine and the hair escaping its braid looked soft despite the whipping of the wind, but there was something impersonal about it all. Someone had given her nice things with no thought for the person they were giving them to.

And then her hand twitched out from beneath her cloak, seeking the threshold, and we all saw the stone embedded in her wrist.

If not for that, she might still have been dead, despite the movement. What the things that roam the countryside might do with a vacant body... but, of course, if the body was empty, the stone would have fallen to dust.

And now we knew what had set the bells swinging.

Great Aunt let her thread unravel and half the Sisters, including the little fool who'd shot the doorframe, went to their knees. Us Mothers and Aunts are too well trained to take leave of ourselves like that, though I confess that in my younger years, I would have been on the flagstones with them. If the casting of that threadspell is the moment of death, its release is the feeling of being seized by a thousand invisible hands and dragged back from beyond. Prickling heat burns like ice through your veins and your muscles clench with such violence that all the blood is wrung from them, then floods back just as abruptly. I was quite distracted by remembering how to blink as Grandmother hauled the girl inside and two of the Aunts – those with the knack for magic always recover themselves quicker than the rest of us –

slammed the doors in her wake.

Grandmother and Great Aunt passed the girl off to Mother Anna and Aunt Grace. There was some question, you see, over whether it was best to place her in the care of a physician learned in medicine or magic, and in the end, it made sense to have both. Anna and Grace took her away to the infirmary, an Aunt went to quiet the bells, and the rest of us were told to go back to bed.

Well, I would have done. I didn't become a Mother by flouting my vow of obedience, you know.

The thing is, I'd just been threadspelled and was not a bit inclined to do as I was told.

Besides, I doubt Grandmother expected anything less. If you'd heard her tone as she said, "Good*night*, Mother River," you could have been forgiven for thinking she was packing an errant child off to school with a warning not to get in too much trouble.

I walked halfway to the dormitories, lagging behind the others. When we reached the stairs, I slipped off down the hallway.

Look at me. Look at my face, look at my shape. I am not a memorable figure. It's very easy for my absence to go unnoticed.

Alas, I am not invisible. Grace, fussing around her patient, caught me hovering in the infirmary's doorway. She nudged Anna, who simply rolled her eyes and said, "Don't know what I was expecting. You might as well come in."

Our new arrival, now swaddled in blankets in the bed by the hearth, was still but for the slight rise and fall of her chest. Up close, I could see the faint glow that outlined her, the light creeping from her pores.

I took the chair beside her and waited until Grace and Anna turned away to discuss something. Then I leaned in, so close that my lips brushed her ear, and murmured, "I know you're awake."

In truth, it was a guess, one that was vindicated by the almost imperceptible tightening of her jaw.

"Don't move," I whispered, then sat back just as Grace and Anna turned around. Grace eyed me suspiciously.

"You're not to bother my patient," she cautioned, ignoring Anna's muttered, "*Whose* patient?" I only smiled.

A little later, when it was established there wasn't much to do but keep the girl warm and wait for morning, I offered to watch over her. They were happy enough to accept, provided all I did was watch, and I swore I would do nothing but keep vigil and let them know if anything changed.

I broke my vow of honesty that night, too.

No sooner had their footsteps faded away down the corridor than the girl sat up, as far from the half-dead thing we'd dragged in from the storm as it was possible to be. Blankets clutched around her, she backed up against the headboard, eyeing me warily.

"You heal quickly," I observed. "Of course you do." And in case there was any doubt as to what I was referring to, I reached out and tapped the black stone in her wrist.

"In the morning," I went on, pretending not to notice the way she had stiffened, "Grandmother and Great Aunt will offer you a choice. They'll ask whether you want to be sent home or claim sanctuary here. Oh, yes." I nodded as her face slackened in surprise. "You may stay. We do not turn away those in need, whatever form they arrive in. We'll keep your body alive and well, and you'll remain as yourself, separate from your Tether." I'll give her this: she tried not to flinch. "Or you can tell us who and where you're from, and we will write to them and I'm sure someone will be sent to fetch you." I gazed at her, taking care to keep my expression neutral. "But as you risked your existence to trek through the snow on the coldest and darkest night of the year, I won't insult you by asking what you want."

She was silent, her eyes fixed on mine. I tilted my head, considering her.

"Tell me," I said, "do you hate your Tether?"

"Hate—!" Her voice cracked, dashed against a rock of indignation. "I adore that child," she said fiercely, and I raised an eyebrow.

"Child? They don't match bodies by age where you're from?"

"They do." The brief flare of anger had quietened. Now she was picking at a loose thread and avoiding my eyes. "She... I was... *we* were a special case." I waited for her to fill the silence that followed, but she'd evidently had that urge trained out of her.

"Tell me about her," I encouraged. "I can guess the basics. She seemed a normal baby, but by the time she was a year old, the light was trying to claw its way out." It's always the way with the Heaven-touched – but of course, you know that. Is it awful, to see it for yourself? To see a baby blessed with a power so great that if they do not use it daily, it burns them from the inside out. To know that if they try to wield it with their own hands, it will burn them from outside in.

After a long moment, the girl nodded. "Her name is Hester," she said softly, "and she was not even seven months old when the power began to show itself. Lady Thorne – that is, her mother – told me it came upon the baby with a terrible violence. The lady is Heaven-touched herself, so she and her husband always knew it was a possibility. They took the baby straight to their priest, but the priest could do nothing. He'd thought as they had: that if the light was going to show itself, it would not be before the child's first birthday. There were no donations available to be made into a Tied."

*Donations.* Such a soft euphemism. Easier for society to swallow. But we know better, don't we? We know what it means for devout families – or dirt-poor ones who can't afford another mouth to feed-to donate to the Church of the Eight Saints. To hand over a newborn and have it raised, unnamed and unloved, until the parents of a Heaven-touched child find themselves in need of an outlet for their infant's lethal power.

"Yet here you are," I mused. "So, someone had their soul scraped out to make room for you. How did the priest manage that, with no donation to hand? Or..." I squinted at her, as though I might spy something of what had transpired. "Were they – your body's original inhabitant, I mean – a martyr?"

Martyr being the Church's word for it. But if you ask me, a grown person who walks up to a priest and asks to be torn from their mortal casing in service of a Heaven-touched is simply looking for a way to die. The Church is supposed to make certain they know what they're doing, that the act is born of true religious conviction. That they have not been pressured or coerced, that they are not seeking an end to earthly suffering.

But when donations are in short supply...

"No." The girl's knuckles were white against the blankets. "If you're rich and desperate, there are...other ways." She flicked a glance at me. "The

Thornes were both."

"The black market?" I had heard rumours of it. She nodded. "Then… " I gestured to her body. "This was not someone who would be missed."

"She was sentenced to hang." Her voice was very quiet. "She was half-starved, so it was hard to be sure of her age, but they guessed she was no younger than nineteen." Old enough to have been a martyr if anyone thought to ask. She tapped the side of her head. "This brain remembers her last moments." Of course it did. Because its original owner had had the chance to grow, to develop a sense of self, to be a person. She'd imprinted an identity on the body, which is precisely why the Church prefers a blank-slate donation to a martyr, for all the Council laud those who give themselves willingly. "They dragged her from the bowels of Spiralgate Prison while she thrashed and bit and howled, and they bound her wrist to the baby's. Hester was wailing. So was she. Her name was Constance," she added abruptly, "though I know little of her other than that. Only that she was filled with rage as they threadspelled her into stillness, and she could not even look away as they sectioned off part of the baby's soul."

The sectioning. Oh, it's a hellish thing, and I do not speak figuratively. The screaming, the smoke, the awful red fluid that reeks like blood and evaporates on contact with air. Thank the angels, I suppose, that the power manifests when the Heaven-touched are so young. If they understood what was going to happen, I suspect most would rather let the light burn them up.

"And then," the girl went on, so low I had to strain to hear, "they clawed Constance's soul out through her wrist." She swallowed hard. "She came out in pieces."

She did not need to tell me the rest. How that separated fragment of the baby's soul had slipped inside the vacant but breathing shell of Constance, stoppered with a black stone formed of her and Hester's commingled blood. How that fragment had expanded to fill the space, and by its connection to the rest of Hester had provided a constant outlet for her light without harming her, giving Hester the chance to grow up and learn to channel the power through it. How, parted from the rest of itself, the fragment had begun to think of itself as its own person, though forever bound to Hester, the Tied to her Tether.

Forever bound. But not necessarily to this body.

I leaned back in the chair. "If your body had died out there in the snow, that little sliver of soul you call *you* would have snapped straight back to Hester and been reabsorbed. They'd have had to find a new body and section her all over again." And there was no guarantee that the soul fragment the sectioning produced would still be *this* girl, but one look at her face told me she was aware of that. "*If* they managed to find one in time, which they may not have done. That's why I thought you must hate your Tether. Why risk it?" And why come *here*? Had she not seemed so shocked when I told her she might stay, I would have wondered what she'd heard about us. "Is it the pain?" I pressed. "Because distance won't make the light hurt any less."

She seemed to glow more brightly as she raised her chin, her mouth a hard line. "No," she hissed. "I'd never have left for my own sake."

"Then—"

"I left," she gritted out, "to save Hester."

Well! If she hadn't already had my attention, that would have grabbed it. I folded my arms. "Go on."

"Constance died despising her." The girl's eyes burned. "Even with her soul in tatters, every piece of Constance hated her. Never mind that she was only a baby. And when Constance was gone, she left all that hate behind, and there's no one to hold it but me. I have spent seven years trying not to act on it!" She blinked rapidly. "Some Tieds, like Lady Thorne's, are barely individuals at all, just echoes of their Tethers. But I am... myself. I am someone who loves that child, not as though she is my own, but because she is more than that. And I am someone with enough mind of my own to know I had to run before the poison Constance left inside me makes me do... something I have no wish to."

I studied her for a moment. "You truly did happen upon the convent by accident, then."

She looked startled. "Of course. When I ran, I had no destination in mind. I was only trying to get far enough from Hester that I could not harm her." Her eyes narrowed. "Why? Why would you ask me that? And what did you mean about your leaders giving me a choice? You are part of the

Church, are you not?" Her voice dropped several octaves, and she shifted closer to me, so close I could hear the hiss of her breath. "Have Tieds come to you before?"

I laughed, right in her face. The sudden noise made her wince, and I was sorry for that, but it was far too funny. "Such a lot of questions! Let me ask one of you: What is your name?"

She stared at me. I waited for the usual nonsense about Tieds not having names, but instead, she said, "I call myself Bluebell. It is Hester's favourite flower."

"Bluebell." I stretched each syllable, letting them dance over my lips. Such a sweet name. Not to my taste, but I could see why she'd claimed it for her own. "This convent is within the Church, you're right. But we are too remote for the Council to bother with very much, so we mostly govern ourselves. A good many of us were not even brought up in the Church but fled here from unsafe homes or places where magic is frowned upon. We even took in the only survivor of the convent at Candle Rise."

Naturally, the name meant nothing to her. If she were local, she might have frowned and told me there were no survivors at Candle Rise. She asked again, "Have Tieds claimed sanctuary here before?"

I smiled. "A lost Tied came to us a few months ago. I recall the weather was a good deal better that day. Poor thing, he barely had a thought or feeling to call his own, just wanted to get back to his Tether. Someone from the Tether's household came to fetch him the next morning. And there was another, before him... she stayed, though the circumstances were quite different. I suspect Grandmother and Great Aunt will tell you all this again in the morning. Then they'll tell you that if you stay, you'll live as one of us, and if the Thornes come calling, we will say that the only people living here are Sisters, Mothers and Aunts, and it'll be the truth, after a fashion." I let my smile stretch until my teeth were bared. "What they will not tell you is that there is a third option."

Before Bluebell could react, I seized her by the wrist. However viciously Constance had fought, the stone had been laid with the utmost care. I traced its outline with the tip of my finger, ignoring the way she shuddered.

"There is a way," I explained, "to sever your connection to your Tether, without harming you. It's not practised much, because the process is quite... volatile. It needs to be conducted somewhere far from anyone – at least, anyone whose life you value. But the method itself is simple. In my experience" —which, granted, was limited, but she didn't need to know that — "it has never failed."

Bluebell was quiet. I could all but hear her mind working away at what I told her, and it worked fast. "What's the catch?" she demanded. "If it's as easy as you say, why would your leaders not tell me about it?"

I gave the stone a light tap. "Well, it *would* kill your Tether. Once your part of the soul you share establishes its independence, little Hester won't be able to cope with a piece missing. I have no idea what happens to the remains of her soul after that, before you ask. She may simply cease to exist." I smiled at Bluebell. "In some ways, I think that's better, don't you? You'd never have to worry about her again. She'd never be at risk of another sectioning, or from Constance's anger. And you'd be free. It's the kindest option for both of you." I stroked my thumb over her wrist. "Will you let me help?"

I will say this for her: she did not give the idea the time of day. The fury with which she jerked her arm away was quite lovely. She did not say no, because there was no need to. I shrugged.

"Oh, very well. I suppose this way we avoid a potential wildfire, for which the local woods will thank you." I stood, pushing the chair away. "You should probably sleep. We rise at dawn, here, and I won't have Mother Anna and Aunt Grace blaming *me* if you're exhausted." They *did* blame me, as it goes, but it's the thought that counts.

I told Bluebell that if she changed her mind, she should ask for me. Then I left.

I heard nothing of her until the next afternoon, after the storm had died down. She had not asked to stay, nor, as you know, had she waited around to be sent home. She'd slipped out some time around noon, while everyone was at prayer, leaving nothing but a note thanking us for our hospitality and expressing her regret that she could not accept the kind of help we were offering. She may have gone north, where the Church does not hold so much power, or east to the places that have little interest in magic. I do not know, and I'm glad of that. I said I'd tell you what I knew. I can't tell you what I don't.

You see, Lord Thorne, I understand that you came here in the hope of fetching Bluebell home. Doubtless, you're worried for your daughter, should something happen to her Tied. More than that, Hester will need Bluebell to hand when she begins to train with her power – when it comes to practising magic, she's essentially useless without her. And even after what I said about the impression poor Constance left on Bluebell, you're sitting there thinking that her love for Hester will prevent her from truly harming the child. Honestly, I think you might be right. Fleeing was merely overcaution on her part.

Still, I take great satisfaction in not being able to tell you where she's gone.

Because I was watching you when I said her name for the first time. You showed not a hint of recognition.

It comes as no surprise to me that you care nothing for Bluebell as herself, only as an extension of Hester, but the fact that I expected as much does not make me any more sympathetic towards you. I have met people like you before. My own Tether's family were the same way.

When I ran, like Bluebell, I came upon a convent. No, not this one. Not at first. It was a hot summer night when I tripped the wards at Candle Rise. Once the nuns realised what I was, they sent word to my Tether's household, but I wasn't going back. Not for anyone. I had spent nearly fifteen years as little more than her power channel, and I loved her, loved her like a twin, like a parent, like my whole world. Yes, she was me and I was but a splinter of her, but at the same time, we were us, and it's hard for anyone who isn't us to understand a bond like that. And yet, that love wasn't enough for me to endure a lifetime as her outlet.

When no one was looking, I had been reading. I'd been listening and learning, until I figured out a way to cut us both free – in a manner of speaking. I didn't want to use it – I didn't even know if it would *work*. I thought perhaps, if I was allowed to live separately from her, I wouldn't have to. But that wasn't to be.

You may not believe this, but I had no idea that this method I'd concocted would be so...incendiary. I was furious with the nuns – I could not claim sanctuary, they said, because I was not a person – but I did not set out to hurt them. I scarcely remember the fire, only being pulled from the rubble by Anna. Sister Anna, as she was then. Someone from Candle Rise had sent out a distress call, but by the time Anna and the others arrived, it was far too late.

The Grandmother at the time was the first person ever to show me compassion. This convent has always been something of a law unto itself, and she told me I was welcome to join. She knew what I was, and she offered me a place regardless. I owe my continued existence to the nuns here.

Run and tell the Council if you like, but it'll be your word against all of ours. You have no evidence. My stone is gone; now that there is no other living body for my soul to return to, I do not need to be sealed up.

I tell you all this not because I have any interest in helping you, but so that you might understand the lengths a desperate Tied might go to. My advice, though you won't take it, is this: Let Bluebell go. Let Hester grow up without the use of her powers, which you no doubt had some self-serving plan for. Trust Bluebell to keep herself – and thereby your daughter – alive.

Don't chase her. You don't want to be there when she discovers the limits of her love.

Now then, about the chapel roof...

Emma Mary Currans is a writer currently based in North East England, an area that inspires much of her writing. At the moment, she is working on a novella, as well as a number of short stories, all within the realm of speculative fiction. Outside of fiction, she occasionally writes poetry, and has previously had work published in *Barren Magazine*. When she is not writing, Emma can usually be found working on her PhD thesis and trying to keep her houseplants alive.

# Dietary Advice

by P.S. Cottier

They believe it happens all one way,
the nutrients running into their feet
through tendrils thinner than thought.
They also use toadstools for recreation,
flying in their minds higher than
any annoying, gossamer fairy,
and they chuckle as they light their pipes.
But the toadstools have their far-from-silly
friends, in those unseen forest fungi,
linking trees by roots, and gnomes,
by their clunking, heavy boots.
Gradually, slower than any slug,
some nutrients change, the recipe thickens.
Before they realise, gnomes can't move,
are wedded to the ground, transformed
to concrete statues. And the process
doesn't stop there. Poria incrassata
performs a tiny, rhythmic dance,
infiltrates the concrete, smothers features
with orange pancake smears.
Each gnome eaten to mere sullen lump,
and the forest laughs, and tendrils flex.

P.S. Cottier lives in Canberra and has published eight books of poetry. She
blogs at pscottier.com.

# Watching the Stars

by Gustavo Bondoni

Ander woke as software, which immediately told him something was very wrong.

His consciousness should have been printed onto a good, healthy *human* body. Instead, he was surfing the ship's database in an attempt to figure out why the computer thought they needed an engineer. Short of catastrophic failure, they should have been able to deal with anything.

"What's happening?"

The ship's main processor responded quickly: "I've received an error message from the colonist storage mainframe which goes beyond my operating parameters."

"Let's have a look."

Ander pulled up some visualisationware to see what the data was trying to tell him. "This can't be right. It's saying that there's no data about the colonists. It's as if all that information is gone."

"That's the way I interpreted it as well."

"But that's impossible. Those mainframes are backed up three times, and each of them is in a different part of the ship. No micrometeorite could have taken out all three. Have you checked the wiring?"

"Yes. I encountered more errors. That was when I woke you."

"All right." He studied the data on the wiring checks and concluded that something must have physically damaged both the hardwired and wireless communication system. That would have taken terrible luck, but it was still more likely than losing all three mainframes. "Let's have a look. Can I get mainframe visuals?"

"No. The video circuits are down to those areas."

Probably the same wiring issue. "Do we have any video that is working?"

The computer presented a short list. Most of the internal cameras were concentrated in the control room and living quarters at the front of the ship – both unused during the automated portion of the flight. A couple of the external ones were promising: one was aligned to show the entire length of the three-kilometre-long vessel. He requested access to that one.

He reflected that it was a good thing that his body was gone, because his blood would have frozen at what he saw.

The ship ended abruptly in a dry-frozen molten mess just beyond the crew area. The mainframes holding the minds of the colonists, the engines, the vast fuel containers – all were gone. The huge space ark was reduced to a small area, designed to sustain a couple of dozen people who would be putting the ship into orbit. It had a small workshop with different types of nanoprinters and held the medical area; there they could live, work and perform their duties. Luckily, the emergency powerplant, a bank of hydrogen fuel cells continuously refilled by ram scoops, was still intact. And those had been designed to keep the entire vehicle running, which meant they wouldn't be taxed by what little remained.

The stars in the image spun crazily. Whatever had caused the damage had also knocked the ship into a dizzying spin.

"Can you wake anyone else?"

"No. I can only wake the crew when we arrive."

"We're not going to arrive."

"That doesn't change my instructions."

"Override."

"You don't have access to that level of override."

"Are there any other engineers in your data bank?"

"No. You are the designated troubleshooter."

"Is there anyone else in this mainframe?"

"No. Just you and the crew."

"Crap."

Ander thought. The issue wasn't one of how to land on a planet or even get into orbit; that was never going to happen. The problem was how to stop himself from going insane.

He asked the computer if he could create an artificial human within the program, to have someone to talk to.

"No."

After some decades of this, and having pretty much memorised the entertainment library, he asked the computer to shut him down.

"I can't do that. I have to keep the engineer active until the problem is fixed."

He raved at it. He threatened it. He tried to appeal to its better nature. But no approach softened the reality of its programming.

Perhaps he could reprogram it himself. He researched programming methods, languages, and security protocols. Once again, he was stymied. The system only allowed the most basic access.

*Ander made plans. The colony needed to be designed, and the original plans were lost with the rest of the ship.*

*So, he learned about terraforming and biology. He read about life support and architecture. He investigated social trends and traffic flow.*

*And he created colonies.*

*He planned beautiful spires that reached towards the heavens, and brutalist bunkers that defended their inhabitants against all the universe could throw at them. He created glittering bands of orbital residences and impregnable refuges a mile underground.*

*And he placed himself inside the simulated images and lived in each one, sometimes for weeks on end.*

Centuries passed. Ander came to see the computer as his enemy. Everything he did was an attempt to thwart its machinations. But he understood that it was a one-sided affair. The computer was unaware of the rivalry, just giving preprogrammed responses to each attempt. Not malicious, but implacable.

*Hope dwindled further. His thoughts, moving at the speed of computer processing seemed to be flying apart, exploding outwards in all directions, never deleted – the machine couldn't allow that – but also never quite coherent. The pressure became extreme.*

*One day, he set a timer. For one century, exactly to the last second, he looked out from the observation cameras, to watch the stars revolving around the ship.*

*When the chime sounded the end of the hundred years, he felt no worse than before. And no better.*


Eventually, Ander understood that he had gone beyond insanity. Only the inherent stability of the program kept him functional at all. His personality and thought processes were exactly the same as they'd been when he was woken – the program couldn't change that – but his thoughts, experiences and memories had evolved so far beyond anything he'd imagined when his personality had been scanned and uploaded that the thoughts he had were not compatible with the way his program was designed to think them.

And yet, everything insisted he was sane. Rational, even.

But sane people don't spend a century – timed to the second – staring at the revolving stars. They don't create detailed maps of a colony destined never to be founded.

Most especially, they probably don't spend all their time composing stories of explorers who come upon derelict spaceships occupied by ghosts who kill them in gruesome and imaginative ways.


*Skarnul the Valorous looked out from the forward viewport of his hyperfighter. The enormous hulk of the ship showed it to be a Terran Megafreighter.*

*He smiled and checked his blaster. "One can never be too careful in these wrecks," he said to himself. "You might find feral animals. Even survivors if the life support remained functional. Better to shoot first and ask questions later."*

*He closed the helmet of his spacesuit and popped the cockpit hatch, blaster in hand and jet pack pulsing...*

These diversions kept him occupied, but couldn't quite satisfy his sense of propriety: he realised that a ghost ship ne eded a dead body aboard. After millennia of silence, he addressed the computer.

"Can I print myself a body?"

"Yes. Each colonist is allowed one."

"Can I download myself onto the body?"

"Only a copy. Your primary mission still isn't done. You need to troubleshoot the problem."

He had the ship print him a brand-new body. It was beautiful: tall, with razor-sharp features and musculature that would have inspired a classical sculptor. He instructed the computer to download a copy of his mind – as it had been when it was uploaded – into that Adonis.

The man attacked the problems logically. The first thing he did was to send out a distress signal.

It was a reasonable thing to attempt. Perhaps other ships were following in their wake. Ander was delighted, however: the odds were astronomical, and false hope would only make the fall that much more painful.

Then, he attempted to get the computer to allow him to create other colonists. But he ran into the same resistance as Ander had: the rules were implacable, hardwired into the system.

Faced with the prospect of spinning alone for decades, the man's discipline broke. He stopped showering, grew a beard, spent most of the day lying on a couch exhausting the ship's library of erotic content.

Then his health began to suffer. He existed on a diet of sugary foods and highly processed carbohydrates, for no reason Ander could see except to flaunt the recommended diet because he felt like it. The muscles turned to fat, the fat to folds and flab. Filthy clothing lay discarded everywhere.

The clone shed the trappings of civilisation, peeling them off like useless bandages, until nothing stood between the reality of the dead ship and the man's battered sanity.

Ander relished watching the man go mad. At first refusing to eat, then bingeing. Running around, yelling wildly that he'd destroy the main computer banks, then hiding in his room for weeks on end. Eventually, he overdosed on something he found in the first aid kit.

It was ideal. In the absence of bacteria, the body didn't decompose – it mummified.

Ander couldn't have planned it any better. Anyone finding them would encounter that gruesome sight sitting there, as if plotting a new course to hell.

Then, they'd discover the little surprises Ander had left for anyone boarding.

All those centuries of learning to program and getting to know the miniscule details of the ship's remnants didn't go in vain. He couldn't wait to see anyone stepping on his derelict ship.

It would give him something to look forward to as the stars went round and round.

Gustavo Bondoni is a novelist and short story writer with over four hundred stories published in fifteen countries, in seven languages. He is a member of Codex and a Full Member of SFWA. He has published six science fiction novels including one trilogy, four monster books, a dark military fantasy and a thriller. His short fiction is collected in *Pale Reflection* (2020), *Off the Beaten Path* (2019), *Tenth Orbit* and *Other Faraway Places* (2010) and *Virtuoso and Other Stories* (2011). In 2019, Gustavo was awarded second place in the Jim Baen Memorial Contest and in 2018 he received a Judges Commendation (and second place) in The James White Award. He was also a 2019 finalist in the Writers of the Future Contest. His website is at www.gustavobondoni.com

# Till Next Time

by A.N. Myers

"So, I don't know if you've heard anything," Jeena said, disappearing momentarily from the screen as she began her pre-hop computer checks, "but the word around Triton is that your job might be going back to automated. Sometime soon. One of the pilots is sleeping with a Space Guild executive, and he told her."

As Jeena settled in her seat, Kent perceived the mottled ochre sweep of Jupiter's horizon reflected in her dark visor. Funny, he'd never noticed that before.

"I think that's unlikely," he said. "Anyone sleeping with a Guild Executive. Your friend would get frostbite."

Jeena grinned at this irreverence. "No, but really."

She has a lovely smile, Kent thought.

He glanced down at the panel which displayed the safety data of Jeena's ship. All within acceptable margins. "As I said, that's unlikely. The Senate would never allow it, nor the pilot unions. The *Renaissance* disaster was only seven years ago. You know the rules; a living person must oversee the checks before sub-light hops. The human touch." He paused. "One minute to launch."

"If it did happen, you could always do something else, couldn't you?"

"You seem very determined to imagine me out of a job."

"It's just that it's so lonely out here. You on your own, Kent, on your little metal island, just Jupiter for company, never seeing anyone face to face, anyone for more than ten minutes."

"I'm not lonely. I've got you and all the other pilots to chat to. And there's Thierry on Waystation B."

"He's two hundred thousand kilometres away in oppositional orbit and you think he's a jerk."

"That's true," he said, laughing. "Anyway, don't let it trouble you, Jeena. Hop in ten seconds."

"But it does trouble me," Jeena said, "I think about you a lot, Kent. I worry about you."

"Well don't. Enjoy Neptune. Till next time."

"Till next time."

He pressed the launch button and Jeena and the ship were gone, the umbilical claws empty. In their wake a dim trail of light from the antimatter engines glistened against the blackness of space. He felt the gravity jolt that always followed a hop quiver through the Waystation. And something else – an emotional jolt, moving him in a way he had never experienced before.

Jeena had been stopping here every week for nearly four years, a face on a screen for an all too brief ten minutes. Suddenly, in that moment, Kent realised that he loved her.

He kept himself busy. Ten to fifteen ships would arrive at the Waystation during a typical twelve-hour shift, chiefly cargo liners, most headed to Neptune's moons, some to the mines of Pluto. Jeena's ship (she was the sole pilot) was a Westley X-6 cargo liner transporting drilling machines and parts to Triton. His job was to run all the safety checks and electronically scan the craft before its sub-light hop. It had been this way since the Senate voted to legislate for human intervention following the *Renaissance* disaster. Malign sentient computer viruses, such as *Mr. Zoltan* and its progeny, had not been fully eliminated from the Guild's systems. Nearly six hundred people had died when *Mr. Zoltan*, for obscure reasons known only to itself, dropped *Renaissance*'s safety shields seconds after launch, flooding the passenger compartment with ambient hydrogen radiation. Hops were shorter now – at least three from Earth to Neptune – and carefully monitored.

Jeena was right though; it was a lonely job. He was like one of those legendary lighthouse keepers they used to have back on Earth, standing guard over the wild spaces, keeping people safe. He would try to keep busy, even when off shift, to distract himself from this isolation; he read a lot, poetry mainly, and had recently begun a degree in viticulture, one of the Guild's free courses. The Waystation had good facilities, too – a small gravity gym, and a virtual entertainment centre. And sometimes he would climb into the silver splinter pod and cruise into the stratosphere of Jupiter, piggybacking the winds and surfing down the troposphere into the bands, where he would behold the awesome beauty of the planet.

Kent would tell himself that this was why he'd stayed so long – here in the Waystation he was poised on the brink of a sublimity that was addictive to his soul. The splinter pod would peel away from the thimble-shaped Waystation and the whole colossal vista of billowing colour that was Jupiter's surface would rise towards him like an approaching friend. This time, he was in the pod just ten minutes after saying farewell to Jeena, he clicked on his safety belt and dived straight down, seventy miles in ten seconds. Even with the gravimetric buffers on, he could feel Jupiter's vast weight pulling him into the chair; he let that great force bring the ship, tumbling like a leaf, down into the interior. The surging winds of colour and gas howled and crashed around him, the ship skipping over them like a stone across a pond. Then the multitudinous forces converged into one magnificent vector which accelerated the ship to a speed of twelve thousand miles an hour.

He switched off the stabilisers. The little craft started spinning until everything through the window became a fractious, glorious blur. The sound – what was it? Not really a howl, more a groan, a throbbing, grinding resonance that vibrated through his bones, growing and growing, deep and loud – so loud – then climbing in frequency to a noise that was almost a colossal yell. The voice of Jupiter, he thought – then he plummeted *upwards, backwards*, the pod's buffers struggling to prevent gravity from smashing him into jelly. After a time, which could have been anywhere between thirty seconds or three minutes, those same pulverising forces spat his whirling ship out into the still blackness of space, into the deep welcoming blaze of steady stars, where he was left gasping with exhilaration.

He glanced at the second gravity sofa. That experience – it was glorious, thrilling – but it was his alone. He shook his head. It was ridiculous to think too much about Jeena, and he was determined not to.

"Computer, take me home."


A week later Jeena was back, and despite his earlier resolution, he found himself telling her about his Jupiter dives.

"That sounds alarming," she laughed. "Nevertheless, I'd love to do that. But we only ever get ten minutes."

"I know. If we ever got a chance, you could come along. It's a pretty profound experience."

"How so?" she asked. She was looking away now at her data readout, and he wasn't entirely convinced she was listening. He spoke uncertainly, as if the concepts he was trying to express were not easily communicable as words.

"It's – well, I guess it's to do with gravity – you can feel the planet working on you even with the buffers on. But – I don't know – down there, in the clouds and the wind, it's impossible not to think of the planet as having a great will of its own, that pulls at your mind as well as your body. It binds you to itself, somehow. When you're in there, you feel part of a greater whole – and it's difficult to get yourself away. There's something... compulsive about it. I'm sorry, I'm not making much sense."

She laughed. "You're not, Kent. But I don't mind. Maybe if you can show me one day, I'll understand."

He felt sad. He knew that that was never going to happen.

"Yes. Till next time, then."

He pressed the green launch button. He hated pressing the button. The dark screen she left behind was as black and vacant as space itself.


Sometimes she would talk about her friends, mainly female pilots like herself, lonely women beating paths across the colossal emptiness of space, living lives of grinding dreariness. They'd meet in Triton bars and chat about Earth, about men, and occasionally they'd have brief, unsatisfactory liaisons with the miners and engineers. But no one had the time to make real relationships. They were always moving.

"It's the way the Guild like us," Jeena said. "Always apart, always isolated."

"I guess that's why they pay so well.' He mulled on this for a second. "I remember how they dug their heels in about staffing Waystations with more than a single person. They kept talking about – what was it? Collusion? They would rather go to the expense of constructing two Waystations than build one with two people on it sharing shifts."

"I've met those Guild executives," she said. "Cold fish."

"They believe that we should embrace loneliness, be abstemious of company," he added. "They're like monks. They think there's something sacred about space travel which is contaminated by friendship." He looked at her image on the screen. She was beautiful to him. "Till next time."

He pressed the button and she was gone.


Another time he made her chocolate muffins in the replicator. He sent them over through the umbilicals. Her face was a picture of utter delight as she stared at his misshapen creations. He thought she might cry.

Two weeks later she sent him a reciprocal gift, in a small pink box with a ribbon. He opened it up and inside, sitting on a crumpled dome of paper, was a sparkling uncut jewel, as big as a baby's fist.

He picked it up and as he turned the gem, it flashed in the harsh cabin lights. "Is this what I think it is? A Neptune diamond?"

"It is." He could hear the pleasure in her voice. "You can't sell this on Earth, of course, if you ever go back there. They're prohibited on the diamond market."

"Coughed up from the very heart of the planet," he mused, still turning the precious object between his fingers. "Hardly a fair exchange of presents, Jeena? A diamond for a bad muffin?"

She smiled, half bashful. "That muffin was worth a million diamonds to me."

Once, Jeena teased him about his hair.

"It's getting long. How do you cut it?"

"There's a robot thing in the shower. I can programme it for different styles."

"That's rubbish. I'll cut your hair if you like."

"You'd only have ten minutes."

"No problemo. There's lots of things you can do in ten minutes." She smiled archly.

This cheeky innuendo filled him with wild joy. It gave him hope.

"Why do you do it?" he'd asked her on another, more sombre, occasion. "This job?"

"Oh. Well, things happened." And then, surprisingly, she opened up. There had been a man who had made her very unhappy. And then, just as she'd shuffled this guy off, her son had died.

"His name was Matthew," she said. "He'd been ill for a long time, since he was born really. His heart."

"I'm so sorry, Jeena."

"I find it easier to remember him, to picture his face, out here, in the emptiness. In space, there's so much room for thought. To make sense of all the things that happened. No distractions. Sometimes I understand those Guild executives."

"Desolate and empty is the sea," he said, half to himself.

"What?"

"It's a poem." He added quickly, "Do you feel it's helped you?"

Jeena shook her head slowly. "I'm not sure." She paused. "What brought you out here, Kent?"

He had nothing so profound to add. He'd followed a meandering path to this still, dead point. At first, he thought he'd just be here for six months or so, make some big money, but suddenly six months had become six years. He was waiting for something, but he didn't know what it was.

"I like it here," he said, trying to justify his inactivity as much to himself as to Jeena. "It's beautiful. And the money is pretty great. I suppose I will go back soon. I always thought I'd like to buy a vineyard in California. But it'd be a hard thing to do on my own. Everything is always harder on your own."

"I know," she said. She was looking at him. He glanced up briefly, then turned his head, afraid almost. He was close to telling her his feelings then, and her eyes had told him that she wanted him to. But he didn't. The story about her dead son made it impossible.

"Till next time, then," he said instead.


How many more 'till next times' would they have, he wondered?

So strange how these multiple brief rendezvous, limited by arbitrary rules, had come to mean so much to him. He lived for these times with Jeena. More and more she occupied his thoughts. He would imagine them together, maybe in a house overlooking a vineyard in the hills; dinner on their laps by a crackling fire, then sitting next to her on the settee, feeling her warmth as he put his arm around her shoulders, laughing, in bed.


Then, all too soon, she was talking to him too quickly, her eyes shining with tears.

"I won't be coming back. Neptune's too far now. The Guild is switching my flight to the Mars hop point."

He'd known this day would come. The unstoppable movement of the planets was wrenching them apart. And he'd never got around to telling her how he felt. Now it would be too late. He wouldn't see her again.

"It's a shame we never met face to face," she whispered, "only through this screen."

What could he say? How could he fill these remaining, dwindling minutes with anything worthwhile? What would even be the point in telling her now? Supposing she laughed at him, told him not to be silly?

"Oh, this is ridiculous!" he blurted out in those final seconds.

"Yes."

He was supposed to press the button.

Now.

But he didn't. He didn't want to.

The ship with its vast butterfly wings stayed fixed between the umbilical claws.

"Is something wrong?" she said, after a silent minute had passed.

"Of course it is. Everything is wrong. Me here, you there, this space between us. Jeena, we're not made for the barren places. People are meant to be with each other. Talking, listening, comforting one another when… well, when bad things happen."

She said nothing for several moments. Her head was bowed on the screen, her hair spilling out from under her grey pilot's helmet. He was acutely conscious of having made a fool of himself.

"I think," she said eventually, "that there might be a fault on the ship."

He felt dizzy. "Why do you think that?"

"I could be mistaken, Kent. But I thought… I thought I saw a red light flash on the console at the end of the countdown. Maybe. If the shields are faulty, the ship could be lost. That's the rules, isn't it? If a pilot even suspects something's wrong, it's got to be checked out?"

"Yes, that's the rules."

"Well, that's what I'm doing. I'm reporting a fault. I can't go anywhere."

She was still looking away from him, pretending to busy herself with the console. He knew that what they were doing was dangerous; the Guild could sue him for everything he had if they thought he was deliberately impeding the progress of a registered cargo liner. But he didn't care.

"I'll put out a call for engineers," he said, dry-mouthed. "Not those amateurs on Europa. If it's the hydrogen shields, we can't take a chance. We'll insist on the engineers from Mars. It will take longer of course, a couple of days at least."

"That makes sense," she said, her voice so quiet he could hardly hear her.

"You can't stay there, of course. I'll come over and get you."

"In the splinter pod?"

"Yes. It takes two. You can… "

"Take me to Jupiter," Jeena said breathlessly.

"Really?"

"Take me around the Great Red Spot, like you promised."

"Of course," he said, his heart racing. "Sit tight, I'm coming across."

Far beneath the motionless ship, the great planet turned, silent and mysterious.

Andrew Myers is a London UK based writer of speculative fiction writing under the name of A.N. Myers. His recent short fiction credits include *The Best of British Science Fiction 2021, BFS Horizons. Sein Und Werden,* and *Cosmic Crime Stories* from Hireath Publishing. His flash fiction has appeared in *101 Fiction, Flash Frontier, Bag of Bones,* and the forthcoming *Valentine* Anthology published by Black Hare Press. His YA science fiction novel, *The Ides,* is available from Amazon. He is a member of Clockhouse London Writers.

# An Informational Plaque Outside the Cathedral of St. Onesiphorus

by Naomi Libicki

Marsh, the builder, worked in stone
Secrets known in ancient Tyre
Royal purple, priestly blue
Arch askew and plunging spire

Therefore, visitor, be warned
Touch the horned and blood-stained shrine
At the peril of your soul
Eaten whole, madness-wracked mind

Marsh's fathers rode the waves
Dangers braved, bore back their fruits
Every fruit contains a seed
Madness breeds; the seeds strike roots

Enter, marvel at the scope
Forsake hope; all sailors learn
Though you land from whence you came
It's not the same when you return

Naomi Libicki writes science fiction and fantasy; she lives in Jerusalem with her husband and kid and makes a mean apple strudel.

# Slow, Slow, Quick Quick Slow
# A Six-Hand Reel to the Music of Time

by Marion Pitman

**1.**

Honour Your Partners

Here on this blade of grass
I poise like a bead of rain,
Like the man on one foot on the tightrope playing the fiddle.
Is a butterfly aware of having a short life?
Or a tortoise of having plenty of time?

**2.**

Pieridine Quickstep

I met a butterfly
Who dreamed he was the Emperor of China
What's it like? I said
Being an emperor?
Strange, he said, closing his wings as he perched for an instant on the edge of a
nasturtium,
The life of a butterfly is short and hard
You burst out of the chrysalis, dry your wings, and then it's a mad rush
Sipping nectar, mating, breeding, before the winter comes.
An Emperor lives for years – I'm telling you, years – and food and drink is
brought to him;
He has many opportunities to mate and breed, whatever the season

And yet
He is not happy.


3.
Chelonian Waltz


Resignedly landlocked, I move slow and steady
Carrying all I own, for fear of loss
Short scaly legs and blunt claws patiently, monotonously, pulling across the ground,
Face at food level, grazing methodically.
When anyone approaches, I tend to pull my head in
And wait till they go away.
Life plods on, I long for hibernation.
But play me music, and I become a turtle:
In music, as in water,
I dance, float, fly,
Freed to move with grace,
Flippers carving a slow arc through the matrix of being
No faster, but lighter,
Just for a moment defying time and gravity's drag.


Marion Pitman has been making poetry since before she learnt to write. A fiction collection, *Music in the Bone*, is published by Alchemy Press. She has no car, no cats and no money; her hobbies include folk-singing, watching cricket, and theological argument. Her very occasional blog can be found at: www.marionpitman.co.uk

# The Emperor's Funeral
by Jon Hansen

Emperor-To-Be Michael Vaughn trailed his family down the aisle at the First Reformed Presbyterian Church of Rosehall Creek before slumping into the front row. His mother wept on his father's shoulder, and even his older brother looked sombre. His grandfather, Emperor Philip (so-called the Terrible), lay in state, casket open. A line of mourners wound past, murmuring in respectful tones as they looked upon the imperial face one last time. Michael ignored them, focusing on what he needed to do.

This was Michael's last chance. Before the funeral ended, he had to touch the old emperor's dead flesh. Even a brief caress would be enough. Then his grandfather's power would pass into him, and he would take the throne. Michael shuddered as he considered what chaos might happen if the old emperor was buried without this taking place: the imperial spark faded and lost, the three realms splintering. Dooms beyond imagining.

"It's okay, buddy," said Michael's father, patting him on the knee. "Be good for a bit longer, and we'll stop for cheeseburgers afterwards."

"I need to say goodbye to Daddy," sobbed his mom. His father nodded and helped her up. Michael rose to follow when a hand seized his suit collar.

"Nope," said his brother. His meaty hand held Michael in place. "Dad said it'll give you nightmares."

Michael struggled, but his brother had three years and several pounds of muscle on him. His mind raced as time slipped away. Then he remembered his grandfather's last gift.

It was a pocketknife with a mother-of-pearl handle. Michael had

picked it up off his grandfather's dresser on their last visit to Shadybrook Nursing Home. He pulled it from his pocket, hoping his brother noticed.

Sure enough, his brother's eyes bulged at the sight. "Hey! Where did you get that?" he said.

He reached out to snatch it away, but Michael was ready. With one quick move he flicked the knife down the aisle to bounce on the carpet. On reflex, his brother let go of Michael's collar and sprinted to get it. Michael ran.

He slipped in line behind his oblivious parents, and then he stood before the open casket. Michael breathed his thanks for this moment. His grandfather had been formidable, ruling the cosmos with his adamantine will. Now he resembled a wax statue, lying in finery amongst the perfume of funereal flowers.

There was a commotion behind him, his brother raging towards him like a vengeful wave. Just before it broke over him, Michael reached out and brushed a finger across the dead emperor's hand.


That night Michael lay in darkness. His parents had confiscated the knife, and Michael had been sent to bed without a cheeseburger. The rest of the house slept with their grief. Still, the emperor cannot be restrained, and he rose to creep down the hall. He entered his brother's room, a silent shadow. Michael considered his sibling's still form as the spark burned in his chest, bright with possibility. It whispered in his head, counselling patience. Michael nodded and returned to his room to plan and dream, of worlds to conquer and vengeance to take.


Jon Hansen (he/his) is a writer, librarian, and occasional blood donor. He lives about fifty feet from Boston with his wife, son, and three pushy cats. His short fiction and poetry have appeared in a variety of places, including *The Arcanist, Apex Magazine,* and *Metastellar*.

# Shadows & Dust

by G.O. Clark


This is a poem
without any clocks,
watches, cell phones
or windup egg timers.

There's a house sized
boulder in the woods next
to where I lived, left behind
by the Laurentide Ice Sheet as
it crept across Massachusetts
and the northeast, containing
stories older than man himself;
time solidified.

For Sunday breakfast,
pancakes with butter and
maple syrup, bacon, and fresh
squeezed orange juice were a
treat, rest of the week cold cereal
or oatmeal, milk and toast the norm,
though Mom always has a 3 minute
boiled egg, salt and peppered, fresh
from the chicken coup.

In the alcove our
party-line phone connected
me to distant lives and places,
to imaginary worlds spinning in my
mind, and even though the conversations
eavesdropped upon, were usually mundane,
it didn't matter; I had nothing more
pressing to do.

I hold time in my wrinkled
hands like a crystal ball, memories
swirling within, everything else
now shadows and dust

G.O. Clark's writing has been published in *Asimov's, Analog, Midnight Under The Big Top, Daily SF,* and many other publications over the last 30 years. He's the author of 16 poetry collections, the most recent, *Tombstones: Selected Horror Poems,* 2022, Weird House Press. His third fiction collection, *Aliens & Others*, came out in 2021 From Hiraeth Publishing. He won the Asimov's Readers Award for poetry in 2001, and was Stoker Award finalist in 2011. He's retired and lives in Davis, CA. http://goclarkpoet.weebly.com

# The True Ballad of Sir Elinore

by Jess Hyslop

I am too old now to be hunting dragons. My arms are wasted, my shoulders ache, and my back jars with every jolt of the horse below me. I have been riding a mere few hours and already my rump burns like a hearth-fire. At least I dispensed with most of my armour. "It'll only weigh me down," I told Margaret when I left. "And besides," I added, mustering my pride, "a true knight does not need a silver shell."

She pursed her lips. She is no fool, my daughter. "At least wear the breastplate," she said.

I grumbled, but I did. It's looser now than it used to be; I've lost the muscle of my younger days. Margaret frowned as she tugged the buckles tight, and then tucked an extra sausage into my saddlebags.

How I wish I were back at the manor now, my daughter at my side, bouncing my grandson on my knee. But instead, I am here, on the fringes of a giant country, picking my way around the lake where once, it is said, Sir Fynot plunged the fiery lance of the Wizard King, ending his reign upon the land. The lake seethed and boiled for three years after, filling the air with sulphurous smoke, and the stink of it drifted for a hundred leagues around. At least, that is what the ballads of Sir Fynot claim.

The lake is still now, and a thin film of algae floats on top.

By the time I make camp that night, my back is stiff as a curtain rod and I can no longer feel my fingers. I groan as I dismount my horse and heave the tack from her back. She looks as tired as I feel, not used to such hard riding. I give her a pat as she chews wearily on her feed. Poor girl. I'm sure

she'd rather be back in her stable too.

Lighting a fire is harder than I remember. My hands shake as I strike the flint, and it takes me six attempts to entice a spark into the kindling. As I boil myself some beans and sausage, I spy a goblin lurking at the fringes of the firelight, its bulging eyes glistening wetly as it ogles my provisions.

"Oy!" I shout, but the dratted thing only creeps closer, reaching spindly fingers towards my saddlebags. It is only when I haul myself up and chase after it, banging my spoon against my frying pan, that it finally scampers away into the undergrowth. I ease myself down again, wheezing. It takes a long time for me to catch my breath.

When was it that I last rode out? Eleven years ago, perhaps twelve? Back when my lady wife – Lord rest her – was still at my side and we were comfortably lodged in my castle. Ah, those were good years. The Queen granted me that place after I slew the great serpent of Innismere. Good stone walls and pretty turrets; a beautiful view over the valley from the eastern tower. Agatha liked that, the view. After she died, I used to sit there and stare out at the curving river, imagining her beside me. *Look, my love, a sparrowhawk,* I would say, *and there, look, an egret* – before remembering I was alone.

Margaret and her husband coaxed me to their manor two years back. "This castle is too big for one old man," she'd said. "And besides, we need your help with Gregory." Gregory gurgled, reaching out for me with his tiny chubby hands. There were bags under his father's eyes.

I grumbled, but I went. It was nice to be nearer Margaret and my grandson, and the manor was cosier than the draughty halls of the castle. Fewer stairs, too, to torment my creaky knees. I still miss the view, though.

Gregory is bigger now, and totters about among his toys like a drunken giant swaying through a forest. He has grown fussy about his food, but I have a remedy for that. I trot his spoon towards him, whinnying like a charger. It makes him chuckle, and he opens his mouth and swallows the gallant steed whole.

Strange to think that it was only yesterday, as I tried to get Gregory to eat his breakfast, that I felt the dragon: the tug at my heart, the calling. It surprised me so much that I almost dropped Gregory's oatmeal onto the flagstones. But I resisted long enough to direct the spoon into my grandson's maw. Then I put him back on his mother's knee.

"I must go." Hauling myself out of the chair, feeling the popping of my spine, the tightness of my shoulders.

Margaret did not hide her dismay. "Oh, Papa. Again? No, you cannot."

I kissed her on the head. "You know I must."

It was true, and my daughter knew it too. I took the oath; I forged the bond. Ah, to be so young again, to be so certain of oneself as to bind one's life to such a service. I did not realise, then, what the cost would truly be.

I have heard of knights who tried to stay. How the tug strained at their hearts, relentless as the passage of time. Every night they dreamed of scales and fur, claws and teeth, and every day they battled the compulsion to leap upon their steeds and ride. So consumed with thoughts of the hunt did they become, they could attend to nothing else: not their loved ones, not their daily tasks, not even care for their own bodies.

Eventually, they went. As we all go.

Margaret did not argue further. Instead, she prepared me well. My saddlebags bulge with provisions: fine white bread, cured meats, an ointment to rub into my joints when they complain too fiercely. As I curl up for the night, cold and sore between the roots of an oak, I savour the smell of her perfume on the blanket she gave me.


My steed is slower on the second day; we plod rather than trot. I do not mind. The gentle pace is all I can stomach. The dragon's tug is not increasing, not stirring into a maddening ache as it can do if I let the beast get too far ahead. Perhaps it too travels slowly, creeping across the land.

Still, I should hurry. Mayhap the beast is slithering towards a castle at this very moment, its nostrils pumping in the scent of a young maiden, ready to snuff out the pride of a noble house. I need to get close enough for the beast to feel my presence, a tug in its own breast answering mine, pulling it away from its potential victims and towards me instead.

But hurrying would mean rattling my old bones within me, and I do not think my back would take the strain.

In the afternoon I spy another knight in the distance. My heart lifts and for a moment I think perhaps he will take the dragon instead; perhaps I can go home. But as he spurs his steed closer, I see the great heads lolling from his saddle. It is not dragons that tug at his heart. A giant slayer, he.

"Ho, sir!" he says, reining in beside me. He is young, not yet thirty. He wears his full plate as though it were nothing.

"Sir," I greet him. I am very aware of my scant armour, my grey beard, the skinny wrists that peek from my jerkin. "Where ride you?"

"Homeward, sir. I have slain the giant Gergatha." He indicates one of the oversized heads. A purple tongue protrudes from its slack lips.

"Well fought, sir," I say.

"And you, sir? Where are you bound?"

"A dragon calls me."

"A dragon?" His gaze travels over me, though he is too polite to comment on my lacklustre appearance. Then his eyes widen. "Why, I know you, sir! I mean, by reputation. Sir Elinore, is it not?"

I blink. "Why, yes," I say. "I am he."

The young knight beams. "I heard your ballads when I was but a boy. They are what sent me into knighthood." He salutes me straight. "Why, sir, I thank you."

"You are welcome," I say, though my heart droops within me like the dead Gergatha's tongue.

"Good luck on your quest," the young knight says. "The beast has much to fear from the legendary Sir Elinore." Though his eyes travel again over my person, and doubt creeps in at their edges. Does he see his future in me, as I see my past in him? I doubt it. Youth seldom sees its path, though age is ever confronted with its own: a trail of footprints, leading back into history, impressions filled with joy and with regret.

I watch him wistfully as he gallops away.

That night I dream I am a bird, circling high above my old castle, looking down at the silver river curling around its walls. There is a face at the window of the eastern tower, but when I swoop down to greet it, it is no longer there. Instead, another bird flies beside me, riding on the air currents just beyond my outstretched wings.

When I wake on the cold ground, my body is so stiff I can barely mount my horse. Yet it must be done; the tug in my heart is taught as a lute-string. The dragon is close, now, and coming closer. I know what that means. It means that I have made it: the beast feels me too. But as I turn my horse's head in its direction, I drift back into the memory of flight.

*Look, my love, a sparrowhawk.*

It brings a smile to my lips as I follow the dragon's inexorable pull.


Late morning, I crest a hill and there it is, coiled in a copse at the bottom of a dell. The beast is long, sinuous, though its scales are dull and scratched, its wings stunted and scraggly. As I observe it, it lifts its head slowly and looks towards me. It has long whiskers and its head-crest droops. Its slitted eyes are clouded; they rove in my direction, but it seems unsure. An old beast then, like me. It looks like it could not crawl another mile, let alone besiege a castle. Still, the calling must be answered.

My steed is not happy about advancing on the dragon, but I spur and bully it down the hill. Then, with not inconsiderable effort, I draw my sword.

The beast heaves itself up, bracing on its two front legs. As I approach it snorts a small flame, but in all honesty, it is mostly smoke. I cough, waving it away. I make a lunge, but my thrust is weak and my blade glances off the dragon's scaled belly. It raises a claw and swats at me, but its eyesight betrays it, and the blow passes just above my head. My horse snorts indignantly. I try another thrust and catch a minor blow, cracking a few scales. The impact jars up my arm, catching me unawares, and in my surprise, I lose my balance. I try to right myself, but the weight of the sword will not allow it. I topple, slowly, off the horse.

Landing in a heap in the grass, I lie winded. The dragon puffs another flame at me, but it merely singes my eyebrows. I pull myself, shakily, to a sitting position. I am bruised. My back complains. I think I may have popped something out of joint.

The dragon noses at me; a tooth dents my breastplate. I grip the ridge of its nostril and haul myself upright. My legs quiver with the effort and there is a sharp pain in my left hip. And yet I lift my sword once more. If I can plunge it into the dragon's eye the fight will be over, but my arms tremble and I cannot raise the tip higher than my waist. The dragon seems to be having a similar difficulty, its claws scrabbling feebly at the ground. Next time it snorts there is no flame, only a noisome stench that belches over me and leaves me spluttering.

Still, we try. I drop my sword and bat at the dragon with my hands while it pushes me with its snout. I dislodge a scale or two; it knocks me down once, twice, thrice. Each time I wish I could rest, but the tug pulls me back up, compels me to try again, to slay the dragon just as the dragon seeks to end me.

After a while, we are both exhausted. I slump against the beast's side. I feel very heavy, and my heart is beating alarmingly fast. Offering a silent apology to Margaret, I fumble with the buckles of the breastplate. Shucking the weight is a welcome relief. Beside me, the dragon lets out a long breath, like a sigh. It lifts its head a little, struggles, then lays it back down in the grass. Together we lie and wheeze.

The tug is subsiding. I would be grateful did not I know why. Raising a shaking hand, I give the dragon's snout a pat. "We answered each other," I tell the beast. "We did what we could." The dragon huffs, perhaps in agreement.

They will write a ballad for this, I am sure. How Sir Elinore and the dragon did defeat one another, foe matched against foe. It will not be false, but it will also not be true. Nearby, my steed grows bored and starts cropping at the grass.

I close my eyes and think of Margaret, of Gregory. I hope she knows better than to set him on the path to knighthood; that when she recites the ballads, she leaves mine out. I hope she tells him instead of the years I stayed with him, how I played with him, how I trotted his food towards him as he squirmed and chuckled. I hope she tells him how, if I could live my long life all over again, I would bind my heart not to dragons, but only to my wife, to my daughter, and to him.

Jess Hyslop is a writer of fantasy, fabulism, and science fiction. Her short stories have been published in venues such as *Black Static, Interzone,* and *Cossmass Infinities,* and her debut novella, *Miasma,* is out now from Luna Press. Jess can be found online at www.jesshyslop.com.

# Order of Service

by Joe Durham

*O**n Entry: the Celebration Choir shall sing 'Heaven's Door'*

He dreamed of a dog. And it got him laid. What are the odds?

*In the beginning was* The *Sign*

They first met in a bar, ridiculously loud. He mimed "crazy" and she laughed. Then he just kind of mentioned the dog. That dog he'd seen in his dream. And she laughed again – she was buying beers for her buddies so she got him one too. And then she heard a song that she liked and she asked him to dance. He'd been working long shifts and this was his first night out in a while; so he was pumped and it was pretty embarrassing because without intending to or it meaning anything, he got hard – just watching her dance.  He wasn't sure what to do, but she made the first move, and they ended up out in the back corridor, behind the beer crates.
    "Christ," she said, "My boss would fucking kill me if she knew."

*There was a time of reckoning in the Garden and a darkening of skies.*

He was on leave from the Orkney rigs, a diver. Making desperate scrabbles for the last of the oil.  She worked out west, Cape Wrath. A role at the Star-

port with some long job title that didn't mean anything. She'd never had a dog, she said. Wasn't likely to get one. They both knew why.

*Lesson: the Guardians assembled for the ascension of the tribes.*

They went to a greasy spoon. He ordered coffee, but she went full Scottish. She talked while she ate, and he watched her. She had some appetite. Her mascara had run a little but he liked her eyes. Boy, could she talk.

"So in Distaff we have to behave like nuns, yeah? Because we got to be tested every day for like a month before take-off, but over in Drone the guys get to party because they don't even know if they're going till the last minute when they do their sperm count tests."

She had ketchup on her chin, he noticed. Great tits, though. They pressed phones and shared numbers and they talked about the future. About how the oil would be gone soon, and so would she. About options.

*First Litany*
*Celebrant: blessed are the eggs*
*Congregation: for blessed is the future*
*Celebrant: blessed is the sperm*
*Congregation: for blessed are the stars*

"As it happens," she said "I'm a science grad, but it doesn't matter a fuck because we're just pet-sitting for the AI on the ships. Foetus farmers. Most of the time we're asleep, of course. Fucking cryo. And most likely none of the embryos will survive anyway."

He nodded. He didn't say much. So she kept on talking; always filled the gaps.

"All the systems are AI, of course, with backups, but it does help if you know how things work."

This was later, much later. He really liked her by now, though they both knew that she was way smarter than him and – let's be honest – out of his league. He was a nuts and bolts guy; you didn't need much math to weld. But she said it didn't matter and there might be a way, you know? To see a bit more of each other.

*Thus it came to pass. Two prophets arose named Recruitment and Selection and they tested the Father and blessed him as good.*

Divers don't ask questions; it doesn't pay the bills. But he liked to listen. And while he listened, while she talked, the planet kept spinning, though its orbit was no longer constant. She talked about Cape Canaveral: gone, the Cosmodromes: gone. Few hopes, futile dreams – a frozen future, either way. The course of his heart was set now. Steady. Irrevocable. She said that she had known right away, that night in the bar. Even before they went out back.

*There came upon the land a time of sorrow, a time to weep, a time to grieve.*

"So they say that cryo feels like getting a general anaesthetic, yeah?" he asked.

She guffawed, got beer up her nose, and then had a fit of giggles.

"Yeah, yeah, something like that," she laughed, "I remember when the first girls got told about this revolutionary new foetal implant technique. 'Not dissimilar to a vaginal douche,' they got told. You can always tell when copy has been written by men."

He gave his I-feel-your-pain nod, though he had no idea what she meant.

"You've got to read between the lines," she went on, "They called it 'cohesive attachment' but I think they meant 'adhesive' or 'invasive' instead of 'cohesive.'

Another nod from him.

"Anyway, it fucking hurts," she said, "and so does fucking cryo."

*And thus it came to pass.*

The cryo tanks on board the Orphan Barclay were brutal. He'd never felt so weak. The drugs that emptied his bowels seemed to drain his soul. They left him gibbering, his core corroded and his belief gone. He would have murdered his mother to escape. But he didn't. And then sleep came.

*Sermon: The text is at the celebrant's discretion, but the theme should consider the importance of luck, providence and fate, as well as concepts of effort, commitment, and the earning of good fortune.*

Luck was what she carried; in addition to the Son. She understood concepts of statistical redundancy and knew the probability distribution of risk involved in their enterprise. Most of all she knew that seven ships was far too few, and that they would need luck to survive. But she also knew that luck wasn't given: it was bought. No one worked longer, thought deeper, fought harder than her. So sometimes she just needed to talk, you know, to let it all out. And for that she needed her rock, her place of calm. Though he didn't say much: that was fine.

*Reading: the Father's poem 'By Any Measure, Many Men Were Better Men Than Me'*

He did not understand concepts of statistical redundancy, and wouldn't recognise a probability distribution if it bit him, but when he decided to go somewhere, he generally went. And when it came to doing stuff with his hands, well that was what he did. And if Atlantic waves would not deter him, well... nothing would. And he didn't play around.

"These fucking software ferrules won't stay fixed." she would say. And he would say nothing; just fix them.

*Second Litany:*
*Celebrant: few ships*
*Congregation: many eggs*
*Celebrant: many deaths*
*Congregation: one future.*

Funny how memory works. Towards the end, the Old Folks couldn't remember which algorithms they had deployed on the previous watch, but they could name all the songs on the jukebox back in the Caley Bar in Ullapool in 2092.

Before the service, we visit the grave sites and place mudsnake-shells by the tomb-ships. The children hold hands as they walk, giving The Sign as they pass the Orphan Barclay, and then enter the ice-cave crypt.

*The congregation will stand...*
*"Praise the Mother" (celebrant only)*
*The congregation shall raise their hands towards the cerulean sky quadrant and the twin moons*
*"Hail the Father" (celebrant only)*
*The congregation will kneel, bow their heads in prayer and give thanks for their salvation and survival on the sands of Tau Ceti IV and speak as one with the celebrant.*
*"And Bless the Dog."*

Joe Durham is a wrinkly recluse and occasional SF writer living on a mountain in Wester Ross (No, the one in Scotland, silly). His hobbies include catching up with trends in Electronic Dance Music and searching for the lost tunnel between the Western Isles and CERN. If he finds anything, he's promised to let us know.

# Spacism

by Debasish Mishra

When my grandfather was my age,
a white knee had knocked a black skull,
he recalls. Colour was important then.

The same way we are told to hate
the aliens from another space now.
They don't belong here – *the others*.

They came to this planet as wanderers
with wonder and wanton spark
and took our shots and wounds.

*Aliens are invisible. They don't exist.*
*They're incapable to do superior stuff*
*like us.* That's what we whisper.

*A poor guy who wanted to marry*
*a reticent alien has been banished*
*from the planet*, Fox reported last night.

And the alien girl was lynched amid
a heartless crowd with mocking smiles
of selfie-maniacs in islands of alien blood

Debasish Mishra is a Senior Research Fellow at National Institute of Science Education and Research, India. He is the recipient of the 2017 Reuel International Best Upcoming Poet Prize and the 2019 Bharat Award for Literature. He was also nominated for the 2022 Rhysling Award. His recent work in speculative writing has appeared in *Star*Line, Space and Time Magazine, Penumbric, Par(AB)normal, Enchanted Conversation, Utopia Science Fiction, California Quarterly, Amsterdam Quarterly, The Big Windows Review,* and elsewhere. His first book, *Lost in Obscurity and Other Stories.* was recently published by Book Street Publications, India.

# The Coming of the Djinn

by Christine Butterworth-McDermott

I carved out this small space
        to plant a seed or two,
just so a trail of nasturtium
could grow like a vine
        to my heart,
the green so bright here in this desert,
I could almost hear macaws.

You looked in through my ivory gate
to see what you could take for free
        or by force. Fanged, you invaded,
ingesting all that you tasted, pushing
your body in, waxy as a worm,
to squat over the delicate tiles.

I tried luring you away with a rat or two,
poked you with a stick, a rake, an axe handle,
then I shifted to fire.
        I tried explosives – but I just singed
my fingers, and cut myself on metal
too sharp to melt.

You remained.

And I learned some curses are meant
to linger, to take root in a sacred space.
But I also learned that if I listened carefully
      I could hear the floor rattle,
an angry ancient melody humming underneath.

There is always a shapeshifter, a beauty maker,
one who, like the gift of thunder, promises rain.
I put my ear to the ground: Yes, it thrums,
*the djinn is coming, large and teeming*
      *with vengeance.*

So, I take a single bloom to press
in a book, a single seed to start anew
and leave the garden all to you.
Go ahead, sit blissful and unknowing,
lick your satisfaction, bake in a false sun,
remain unaware. I already know
retribution is slithering there.

Christine Butterworth-McDermott is the author of two books and two chapbooks of poetry. Her fiction and poetry has been published in such journals as *Alaska Quarterly Review*, *The Massachusetts Review*, *Revolute*, and *Voyage*, among others. From 2013–2022, she was the editor of Gingerbread House Literary Magazine. Her forthcoming collection, *The Spellbook of Fruit and Flowers*, will be released in 2023.

# The Camera Trapper

by Alice Hughes

### Camera 1

A fox and her cubs, recently born. They have made a home in the hollow of a sweet chestnut tree. The cubs tussle with each other in the long grass. The mother noses them forcefully to break them up. She licks their fur clean.

### Camera 2

A steely still heron sits on the bank of the mere. He begins skulking the water for fish, and catches one at lightning speed with his long beak.

### Camera 3

A deer? No, far too upright. It is a human. What are they doing out here so late in the evening? They are too far away to make out their features. They blur into the hedgerows. The shot is from one of the traps I put beyond the boundaries of the reserve, to see what is passing through.

Whenever I take the memory card out of a camera trap and insert it into my laptop, I feel like I'm a boy again on Christmas morning. You never know what you are going to get. Camera traps help us see what the human eye can't. When the warm body of an animal moves past the infrared sensor, it causes the camera to fire, recording an image or video to my memory card. The traps are small boxes strapped to trees, logs or fences, that sometimes attract a sniff or nudge, but never disturb animals.

Once, Rosie and I set up traps together. Hers captured enviable shots

of a booming bittern; the shy, rarely-seen birds that hide in the reed beds. As I watched her present them to families and kids on our show and tell evening at the reserve, I felt so proud. "Your nature nerdiness is rubbing off on me," she said, spooning me in bed that night.

"Your free spiritedness is rubbing off on me," I turned to face her. "I love you, Rosie."

After checking all the camera traps, I walk back to my car. The moon is a curved sewing needle in the sky. Chill air pricks at my feet and hands. Even under gloves my fingers and knuckles will be bleached from Raynaud's syndrome. I get it whenever I'm cold, anxious or stressed. It means I can't go cold water swimming with Rosie. She's been going more often at weekends without me, and to evening classes during the week.

Rosie is at a class tonight. I get home and make a vegetarian lasagne for dinner – Rosie's favourite – and leave her a note to say help herself. In bed I read a paper on the development of fen carr on the reserve. I drift into sleep and dream of getting trapped in a tangle of low bent mossy, lichen-furred willow. A camera trap watches me as I sink into boggy peat.

I wake, reaching for Rosie. She murmurs. I stroke her red hair and find something dry: a leaf. I pull it out and put it on the bedside table.

Sunday. We share croissants and my homemade jam for breakfast. I notice her clothes are in the washing machine. Her walking boots are caked in mud.

"All your things are so muddy, love."

"It was ramblers club last night. We went a bit off route," she smiles. "You know I love going off route."

For the rest of the day, she shuts herself in the study and writes folk songs for her guitar. She hasn't been sharing them with me lately. I make a wild mushroom stir fry for dinner. I bring her up a plate and knock on the door. She thanks me and says: "I won't be too much longer."

I lie in bed and scroll through the news. I try to stay awake and wait for Rosie, but my eyelids are heavy and I surrender to the mattress. I am woken by a chant, an incantation, the same name over and over. I am forced to listen as Rosie repeats his name softly in her dream: David. David. David. It's the first time this has happened. I don't admit it to her openly, but she knows I don't like to hear her talk about him. David wasn't only Rosie's old boyfriend. He was my friend. I always find an excuse to put off the conversation, or a reason to leave the room. Now, I am paralysed under the duvet.

A week passes. I don't mention it. I drive to work in the rain and squelch around the reserve in my wellies to collect my camera traps. I turn on the electric heater in my office and check the traps.

**Camera 3**

Shot after shot of a fat tongue licking the camera. It belongs to one of the Highland cattle that graze the land.

**Camera 4**

A short-eared owl flies low and rests on the bank of a ditch, looking for scurrying mice and rats. Her yellow eyes – turned ghostly white by the night – stare at the camera.

**Camera 2**

Is that really a woman? I rub my eyes, and look again. The woman slips off the wooden platform into the mere, just outside of the reserve. She has Rosie's tall triangular figure, her broad shoulders, her skinny hips and long legs. I recognise the daisy pattern on her swimming costume. Rosie does swim here sometimes, but why is she swimming so late? I click through the shots. Rosie swims around the water lilies then rolls onto her back and floats, looking up at the stars. Something large and dark rises from the water. An old boat, a piece of driftwood? It is covered in weeds. A branch blows in front of the camera and blocks the view.

The next morning, I make us a cup of tea and stare at the washing line in the garden. Rosie's daisy swimming costume is hanging up, swaying in the breeze.

"How was last night?" I ask, realising that I have snagged the tea bag in my mug.

"It was nice. I went for a swim at the pool. It was gloriously empty. I had a whole lane to myself."

"You wouldn't fancy going wild swimming at night would you?"

"No, why do you ask that?"

"It's just... On one of my camera traps outside the reserve boundaries, I caught a shot of a woman swimming earlier this week. Pretty crazy, right?"

"That's creepy, Cian. So now you're spying on women?"

"Not intentionally," I sigh. She leaves the room.


A week later, I find several of my cameras – including the one by the mere – smashed up and clogged by river weeds. For several nights, I can barely sleep. I think about confronting her. I fear it will push her away. It was probably just some bored kids.

Tonight a strong wind bangs against the house. I hear Rosie shout goodbye. She says she's heading to the pool, but what if she goes to the mere in this? I sit for a while longer on the sofa biting my nails, then put on my coat and get in the car. I drive towards the mere.

Dusk paints everything murky grey. I put up my hood, but the wind still slaps my face. It begins to rain heavily. I shine my torch towards the mere. In the distance, a huge looming shape – something alive – moves towards Rosie as she swims breaststroke. It looks like she is heading towards it, pleading with it to engulf her and drag her down.

"Rosie!" I shout, running towards the bank. I slip over and graze my leg, then stumble up. "Rosie, get out of there!"

I reach the boardwalk and keep shouting. She looks up at me. Under my torchlight, her face is calm and content. The wind softens, the rain lightens. "It's David. He's come back," she says – elated – swimming towards me with the thing, the beast. It hauls itself out of the water onto the boardwalk and kneels. It does have David's bear-like body, but I can't make out an inch of skin under the dripping weeds. Bile creeps up my throat as he reaches his hand down to Rosie. She takes it and he pulls her out of the water onto the boardwalk.

They never did find David's body, only his rucksack: waterlogged and ripped by the storm that day.  It must have been lurking down there all this time for nearly a decade. Last night, we washed him in the shower and dressed him in some of my clothes. Somehow, he is still caked in soil, stagnant water, goose poo and claggy weeds – the river has become a part of him. The stench of him seeps into the corridor as I walk past and sneak a glance through the ajar door of the spare bedroom. Rosie is sitting on his bed, stroking his tangled black hair, singing one of her songs to him.

I go downstairs and stare into a black coffee. Eventually, Rosie comes down and joins me at the kitchen table.

"He's going to sleep for a while longer," she says. "The day he went missing, I was meant to meet him by the river. But I had to cancel at the last minute. I'd had a nightmare day at work. My head was pounding. If I'd been there, this wouldn't have happened."

"You can't torture yourself, Rosie. It might not have made any difference."

I reach out to stroke her arm. She flinches away.

"Do you know why he did it?" I ask. "I can't imagine just giving up like that." I nearly add 'or choosing to leave you.'

"You're as bad as the villagers and their rumours. No one knows if he meant to drown. The storm came from nowhere that day. And anyway, it wasn't exactly a choice. He was ill. I thought you understood that."

I try to open my mouth to say that I do understand, that I am sorry, but she is up before I can. "I need a nap. I'm exhausted," she sighs.

"He was my friend too," I murmur as she leaves the kitchen.

While they sleep, I think about the times when David and I would go to the pub every Friday to play pool, sing badly to Fleetwood Mac or recite lines from our favourite films. Too many times I got too drunk, and David walked me home. He was reliable, kind, loyal – I always looked up to him, like a big brother.


Every night, I hear him moving around. He does not speak. More bits of him escape each day; they smother the walls and slither under the doors.

He leaves shallow water in the spare bedroom where water lilies rest, whirligig beetles skim and great-crested newt tadpoles swim. Everywhere I go I knock into emperor dragonflies and blue damselflies. Sometimes, I see him reach his hand into the water, slip a freshwater mussel into his mouth, then lick his lips.

Rosie often wakes in the night to go and check on him. There is no escaping the looks she gives him. Tonight she lingers in his bedroom. When she returns, she curls in a foetal position – as close to the edge of the bed as she can get. The distance between us lengthens: a bottomless cavern I can't cross.

"Maybe we should call the police and tell them he's been found," I suggest.

"I'm not sure it's him though, is it? It's not the David everyone will know. It's just – I don't know – part of him. He's inside there somewhere, but he's not... he's not fully himself."

"He's not fully human," I mutter.

She glares at me. "We can't tell the police. They'll take him to some government lab and do tests on him like he's an animal." She turns away from me again. "I'm going to sleep now, Cian. I'm tired."


I wake in the middle of the night. The water has spread to our bedroom. David has woken up again. His footsteps thump and echo, making the walls shudder. He will kill me, if I don't kill him first. He will suck me in and trap me inside to devour later, like the bladderwort spawning through the house. Or worse, he will steal Rosie away and drag her down to his watery lair.

I reach across the bed and find empty space. My heart lurches. Where is Rosie?

I get up and put on my wellies. David is moving high in the house. I realise he must be in the loft. He is searching for something. I should never have taken it. I should never have kept it.

By the time I reach the loft, it is too late. David is sitting on the floor reading his diary, his dark eyes slick with tears. Rosie is sitting beside him, stroking his back. She glares up at me.

"Why is his diary here, Cian?"

"I don't know I—"

"Don't mess with me. It was taped up in this box."

"It's complicated," I sigh. I tell her the truth – or at least half of it. How I found the diary on the day he went missing. I took it before the police got to it.

"That could have been evidence. Why did you do that?"

"I didn't remove any pages. You can see for yourself. I'm sorry, I just – I didn't want to lose it. It's all I had left of him. The last entry, it's – it's for you."

David passes the diary to Rosie and as she reads the last pages, she weeps. He puts his arm around her. I leave them to it.


At work, I reposition my camera traps. My mind whirrs. Guilt curdles in my gut. I'd met Rosie briefly at a few parties with David, but I'd never known her until I read his diary. His feelings poured out for her on the pages, in a way they never did out loud. I ended up chatting to her at his funeral. We exchanged numbers.

Without the diary, would Rosie have liked me in the first place? Would I have known to talk to her about heavy metal bands; taken her to see foreign films at the cinema; asked her about her childhood, her dreams, the songs she wanted to write? To never raise my voice or criticise her, the way her parents did. To make sure when she moved in, she had enough space in the house to practice her music undisturbed. To always prepare her for surprises. There are many other things about her I learned myself. It wasn't long before I didn't need the diary at all. But I still can't get it out of my head. I guess that's why I've kept it boxed up for so long; I worried that if I got rid of it, she would leave me.


Usually, they spend each night together reading the diary. Tonight, Rosie has a migraine and goes to bed early.

"Let's have a drink, like the old days," I suggest to David.

I keep refilling his glass, and pretending to drink from mine.

"You always called me a nature nerd. I was in awe of your carpenter's hands. You would whittle the perfect birdhouse, then ask me to help you name the birds that fed there."

He smiles and nods, but does not speak. He turns his diary to a page about us: a memory of our birdwatching trip where we saw a marsh harrier carrying mice to her chicks. After a while, his attention drifts. He lingers on the last page of his diary – the letter he wrote to Rosie but never delivered. My fingers are turning white; soon my whole body will be bleached pale and bloodless. David looks suitably sluggish and drunk. I try to grab the diary from his slimy hands. He won't let go.

"Stop," I breathe, letting go, noticing how the room is filling with fast-flowing water. "Rosie is here. It'll drown Rosie too."

He looks up at me; I see my flushed, shaking self in his dark eyes. After a while, he eases his grip on the diary, lets me take it. The water drains away. I remember when we would play cards or pool; he was always better than me, but often let me win. I step away from him. He backs into the corner of the room, hunches over and holds his knees. He looks down at his empty hands.

"I'm sorry, David. I'm so sorry," I say, but he has his head in his hands and doesn't seem to hear me.

I find a pen and write my apology on a blank page in the diary. I hand it back to him. He reads it and reaches out his hand for the pen.

"Take me home," he writes.

When he stands up, weeds, reeds, rushes and darting slithering creatures return to him in a frenzy. He soaks them up into his hulking body, then walks towards the front door.

I wake Rosie. She looks at me with bloodshot eyes. "I'm so sorry I took the diary, Rosie. I did it without thinking. I'd always been curious about what he wrote in there. And then I started reading about you... and well, when I met you, I understood why he loved you so much."

"I can't forgive you for it, Cian."

"I know."

"Where's David?"

"He wants to go home, Rosie. Shall we take him? Or did you want to go alone?"

"But it's so soon," she croaks, jolting up.

We put on our coats. Rosie sits with David in the back of the car, holding his hand, singing to him. In the rearview mirror, I see him rip out a page of his diary and hand it to her. She puts it in her pocket.

We reach the mere. Before David descends, I notice he has a page open about Rosie. They are reading it together. She laughs and weeps. He closes his diary, holds it close to his chest, looks at her one last time, then dives down. She stays in the water for a while, surrounded by the bubbles of surfacing fish and thin lines drawn by pond skaters.

I drive us home. She sits in the passenger seat with a towel around her shoulders. I turn the radiator up to stop her shivering.

"I hope he won't be too lonely," she says, wiping away a tear.

"Me too Rosiekins," I say. It's the nickname David used for her. "We can visit him, whenever you want." You'll always love him most. And that's okay with me. I loved him too. It's okay, as long as I get to love you."

Alice Hughes is a writer, comms manager and nature nerd living in Cambridgeshire. She received her MA in Creative Writing from Goldsmiths University and is an alumna of the London Library Emerging Writer Programme. She is currently working on her debut novel and short story collection.

# A Rock and a Light

## by Anna Ziegelhof

The little planet trembled when a machine crashed on its night side. Marieke's lander had caused a similar quake, some time ago. By now she was a familiar unknown, with her quirky dreams and her meek reliance on the planet's resources.

Her heart began to pound like it always did when she perceived an unexpected noise. She left the cabin she had built in the little planet's verdant forest and took her heavy weapon with her.

Sometimes she took the weapon apart, placed its parts on the ground, cleaned each part thoroughly, and put it back together. From the weapon, the planet had learned a lot about the war and about Marieke. She had been expecting someone to come for her. After her arrival on the planet, she had spent a lot of time cowering under a tarp. Only after nobody else had landed on the little planet for a long enough time had she built a cabin in the forest. They'd had a tranquil life until now.

Marieke snuck from tree to tree. The intruder's lander had crashed in the tiny desert, the sand pit Marieke had persuaded not to bring back memories of the war anymore.

Marieke stopped where the soft forest floor turned into grainy sand. She made sure a tree stood between her and the new machine. Her breathing became very shallow. But her heart, her heart knocked heavily against her ribs. The piece of foreign rock she carried in a silver cage on a chain around her neck bounced a little in the wake of each heartbeat.

All was quiet as the dust settled. A lander, exactly like Marieke's. No wonder Marieke often saw herself confusing friend and enemy in her nightmares. It must have been difficult to know against whom to use that

weapon of hers.

The lander had settled in the sand pit lopsided, sinking into the planet as if it were tired from its flight. Eventually, its hatch was released: there was hissing and sighing as the lander and planet negotiated their atmospheres. Marieke's breathing stopped entirely. Only her heart now.

A new speck of light appeared on the planet. The person who emerged from the lander carrying it. It illuminated the planet's night softly. It wasn't at all like Marieke's harsh beacon that she sometimes charged by capturing energy from the planet's sun. This was a small, contained flame.

Marieke readied her weapon. With a quiet click, the gun recalled its purpose. When the new arrival heard the sound, she reacted immediately, by staying perfectly still, like a scared animal, but her flame kept dancing, oblivious to any danger.

Marieke tensed and aimed her weapon. The planet disagreed: killing was not acceptable, even if it was to defend their peace. While Marieke hesitated, the stranger raised her hands. The light she had brought with her moved upwards and illuminated her.

"Affiliation!" Marieke demanded.

The stranger uttered a strangled sound of indecision. Marieke moved toward the sand pit.

"Identify yourself!"

The vibrations from Marieke's vocal cords caused a reverberation that echoed off several landmarks on the little planet, including the new lander and the new person and her luminous artefact. Marieke snapped her bright light on, the one that harnessed the power of the planet's sun. Its beam dwarfed the stranger's modest flame.

The new person finally spoke. She recited a designation. She was weak. The little planet pushed her to her knees without meaning to. She knelt in its sand. Some of the grains surveyed her wounded skin. Those burns hadn't been inflicted more than eight of the planet's short days ago for humans that was a long time to go without food, impossible without water.

"...but I left the war," the stranger added.

"Deserter!"

Four of Marieke's gasping breaths passed before the new arrival affirmed the accusation.

The curious lantern with its flame stood in the sand now, its emanations overpowered by Marieke's violent beam.

"Are you hurt?"

"There was a mine."

"So you thought 'fuck this,' took a lander, and looked for an uninhabited piece of rock?"

"Yes," the stranger said.

Marieke switched off her bright light and allowed the stranger to see her by the dimmer light of that lantern, the stars, and the planet's waning moon.

"Me too," Marieke confessed.

She let the new arrival fetch her pack and secure her lander. She led the woman back to the cabin in the forest. She showed the woman the shallow pool by the river. The noises the woman made when the river water touched her wounds sounded like one of the planet's small nocturnal predators.


The woman's name was Neri, she told Marieke. She brought her light into Marieke's cabin. She also brought tension with her and fear, even though she had been offered water and now a meal and shelter. They were sitting across from each other at the sturdy kitchen table Marieke had built from one of the planet's trees. Neri's striking artefact – her lantern – stood between them on the tabletop, somewhat closer to Neri than to Marieke. The lantern gave them information about each other: facial expressions and outward appearances for now.

Marieke's hair had grown back after being shaved in the war. She had been away from the war for twenty centimetres of hair. Neri was still bald. She weighed somewhat lighter on the planet than Marieke.

"You deserted, too?" Neri asked.

"I stole a lander. I have been travelling for a long time. This is where I have stayed the longest so far. It's a peaceful place."

"I deserted eight shifts ago," Neri said. "Just been hiding behind rocks and little planets."

"What's your plan? Not to wait out the war? That'll be your whole life."

"To wait out the war," Neri said.

The lantern flickered on the table between them.

After they had eaten, Marieke suggested extinguishing its delicate flame for the night.

"No. Not again," Neri said.

Not again?

An awakening stirred in the room, not of an organism but of a slightly ensouled object. It was the lantern that shook off its contemplation of the present, the table, Marieke, Neri. It carried a past in itself, just like the humans. But its past was too heavy and too long for a small object such as itself. Its memories weren't as agile as those of short-lived humans and not quite as vast as those of the little planet. As the lantern startled awake on the table made of the planet's wood, there was a spark of recognition: there was another object here, slightly ensouled, that had lain dormant too. There was a minute warbling of molecules and memories in Marieke's kitchen. The two objects the humans had brought to the little planet began to sense each other. They began to sing to each other on a frequency known only to observant objects. They wished to remember each other, but they didn't quite know where to begin. In the present?

"What's that thing around your neck?" Neri asked during a bath in the planet's river.

"Piece of rock from Earth."

Marieke turned away, hiding the Earth rock from Neri's probing questions.

Why wouldn't Marieke share her memory out loud? She had dreamed it into the patient atmosphere of the planet so many times.

"What's with that thing?" Marieke challenged Neri at night when the lantern spread its glow through the cabin.

"It was my mother's."

Silence fell.

The little planet had learned something: two humans couldn't read each other as well as it could read them. The humans had learned something too: they shouldn't have asked casually about those delicate objects. The humans had hurt one another by asking too harshly too soon. There was a sad closing up of those intriguing things, a pulling back into their previous dormancy, right when the awakening objects had been about to gain some insight into their past, recent or distant. This was not the way forward in remembering. But the objects were old, and they had time and they decided to rest for a while and let the humans progress at their own bumpy pace.


Marieke and Neri spent their time sleeping, eating the planet's produce that Marieke cultivated, and talking about superficial commonalities: factions, units, operations. They carefully excised stories about what blood looked like when it gushed into the desert sand of that embattled planet. What wounds smelled like. What death sounded like. At night, however, those disregarded stories came out all on their own in their nightmares.

By the calm light of the lantern, Marieke tapped across the wooden floor of the cabin. Neri had been whimpering in her sleep, so Marieke gently brought her out of her dream. Neri surfaced from the war with a yell that made Marieke twitch. It took minutes for Neri's tears to dry, her breathing to still, her jaw to unclench.

By the light of the lantern, Neri followed Marieke from her cot to Marieke's bed and they spent the rest of the planet's night close to each other, reminded, even in their sleep, of the safe heat of another living being right next to them. That became the way they slept every night from then on. Humans were better suited to comfort other humans than slightly ensouled objects, the rock sang to the lantern, which agreed.


"What made you desert?" Marieke asked.

The rock startled. The flame fluttered. Why ask such a question, all of a sudden, in that particular, otherwise insignificant moment, while cleaning the planet's vegetables brought in from the vegetable patch? Perhaps it had been the preceding days of tranquillity during which not too much anxious energy had sped up their heart rates and not too many dire memories had caused their rest to be disrupted. The objects were alert. This could be it, they thought: the moment in which the humans began to share important memories; the unravelling of the mystery of their acquaintance.

"The list of the dead had become too long," Neri answered, accepting a cleaned edible root from Marieke.

"The first entry on the list was my grandparents. They had spent their lives' savings to buy places on an evac ship to escape our planet. They got on and the ship was blown up. We had stayed behind only because my father called himself a patriot. The second entry was my father. He joined the war to defend our planet. Our planet hasn't even taken a side. It's just in the way. So, I grew up with my mother. She was too scared to move most of the time and wasted her precious life that way. My mother was the third entry. She went to fetch water and got caught in a blast."

"So you joined the war."

"Like my father before me."

"Like my father before me," Marieke echoed.

"Where else to go?"

"Where else indeed."

"And you?"

"Lieven's death did it," Marieke said. "We had fought together. He died next to me. It's wrong of the war to teach a person that it's best not to love."

They continued scrubbing the little planet's soil off the roots they were going to cook for dinner.

"He gave me that piece of Earth rock you asked about the other day," Marieke said.

The rock rejoiced and sang to the lantern. The humans had finally begun to tell their stories.


"What does it say there, on your pendant?"

"It mustn't stop with you," Marieke translated from the language that she sometimes used in dreams about her Lieven who had died. "Lieven always carried it."

Marieke spoke quietly. The sound waves were cradled by the planet's air and reached both objects and they listened.

"It had been his father's. One of their ancestors had brought it with them from Earth. It was handed down in his family. Both Lieven and his father died in the war. After the mine went off and before he died, Lieven handed the rock to me."

"That bullshit war," Neri recited their frequent mantra. "What do you think it means, 'it mustn't stop with you'?"

"Lieven once told me its story. I don't know if it's true, but I want to honour his traditions."

"Even if they are not yours?"

"He made them mine. He connected us, by loving me and by dying, and by leaving me this piece of rock as the only thing I have left of him."

"What was the story?"

"In his ancestors' village on Earth, there was a sacred building. The villagers committed a terrible atrocity against those who worshipped inside the building. Those who were able to escape never came back. So the building stood abandoned in the village for many years. The atrocity had been so grave that the guilt of it haunted even the villagers' descendants. They knew the sins of their ancestors could never be forgiven, and they vowed perpetual repentance: they decided to care for the building that wasn't theirs. They passed down custody of it and reminded each other of their crime and their responsibility. They treasured the building, as a warning, as a symbol, as a memory, as well as they could. When they had to leave Earth, they took what remained of the building with them."

"You carry someone else's sin?" Neri asked.

"Along with my own, I suppose. The things I did in the war... And why? Because someone told me to? The responsibility mustn't stop. The memory mustn't stop. That's what I think it means. That's what it means to me."

It was quiet in the room. The rock shivered. Marieke had touched its ancient memories.

"And you?" Marieke asked Neri. "An archaic lantern with a live flame?

In need of fuel, in a war about fuel?"

"The strange thing is," Neri said, "it hasn't needed fuel since I lit it."

"There's still space for miracles in this awful universe?"

"I had been disinclined to believe that too."

Now the lantern stirred. It hadn't been difficult to stay lit, it thought, it was its calling.

"The lantern was the only thing I took with me when I joined the war after my mother died," Neri told Marieke. "It was hers and her parents before that. I often begged her to light it when we were hiding in a dark dugout under our house and the impacts came closer and closer. She always refused. Her parents had taught her that once lit, it must not be extinguished. I think my mother had a hard time believing in permanence after my father died. She couldn't bear the responsibility of being the one to relight the lantern and possibly seeing it extinguished again."

"But you could."

Neri made a sound in the gentle dimness of the lantern, half sigh, half chuckle.

"You see," Neri said, "it's not my own permanence I believe in. This artefact has endured for generations. I don't even know where it came from. Fire endures in all the suns we know. Its permanence reminds me of my own impermanence."

The lantern marvelled and it sang to the rock about its awakening memories: before the lantern was extinguished, it had witnessed many lives. It had witnessed singing and solemnity; new babies coming of age and having babies of their own and dying much later. Then came a period of darkness to which the light, deprived of its calling, couldn't testify. A hazy period of travel, of changing atmospheric pressures, of unseen noises and changing voices, and many different languages. Its most recent memory was of being handled gently and being lit again. Its awakening glow fell upon an injured young woman. She was all alone in a floating chamber, illuminated by stars and control panels. "Bullshit war," had been the first words the young woman, Neri, had spoken in the light's presence. Soon after that, the light had been brought into the presence of the rock on a little planet. Once, aeons ago, they had known each other. But the rock had had to stay while the light had been taken away.


Before morning broke after that night full of awakening memories, lightning crashed down from the sky of the peaceful little planet. Marieke and Neri rushed outside and covered the crops in the pelting rain.

The atmosphere of the little planet shuffled its molecules. Lightning sent charges through the lantern, which flickered, and the rock, which didn't split, and when Marieke and Neri arrived back at the cabin, dripping and exhausted, the rest of a backwards-told story was waiting for them there, between them and all the other slightly ensouled things that the little planet had come to think of as, somewhat, its own. The planet's swirling electricity had made their connections more conductive and even after the charge fizzed out, memories stayed blended and invigorated:

Once upon a time, the rock and the lantern had been part of the same sacred building. The lantern had illuminated the activities of its dear community, the rock had held up an ornate ceiling above them until dark days dawned. On the night of the fire and the screams and the shattering glass, those who fled came to fetch the lantern, but they had to leave the rock behind: it rested solidly, even after the attack, as one small part of their cherished building. The rock stayed and mourned, and the lantern was extinguished during its keepers' gruelling flight. At some point in history, each had dozed off. The weight of the years had become too heavy.

The lantern showed Neri its memories of fear and death, world-shattering disbelief and despair.

The rock showed Marieke its memories of the unheard pleas of the innocent and unhinged violence.

Marieke's trembling hands reached for the closure of the necklace. She unhooked the chain and took off the small weight of the rock. She gave the rock to Neri, and it made the lighter woman into a somewhat heavier presence on the planet, somewhat graver and somewhat stronger.

"We tried," Marieke said, the echoing whisper of generations of humans in her small voice. "We took care of your building as best as we could. One day the building collapsed, but we took care of its ruins. When we left the planet, we took care of this last piece, still hoping to return it one day. Here it is now."

And so, the rock and the lantern were reunited at the kitchen table made of one of the planet's trees. The objects cried and rejoiced, free to dream of the future: before Neri would wake from fitful sleep, Marieke would sneak out of the cabin and move swiftly through the forest to the place where her old lander rested. The lander had stood there, hidden, for so long that the little planet had forgotten about the indentations it had left in its forest's ground.

The wet tarp would slide off the lander's surface with a hiss.

The reposing vehicle had sheltered Marieke against many hostile environments before they had arrived. Soon after their arrival, it had ceased all transmissions and become very quiet, deciding that it wasn't going to risk revealing the planet or Marieke to anything scanning the sector for stolen goods, human or vehicular. It, too, had seen enough of the war.

Marieke's hand would touch the lander's access ladder, one of her feet already settled on the bottom rung. But Neri's running steps were going to disturb the quiet of the early morning in the little planet's forest.

"What are you doing?" Neri would use the war-voice she often used in her dreams.

"Atoning," would be Marieke's answer.

Neri's hand would come to rest on Marieke's, halting her movement.

"Don't run away," she might say. "This is a new memory. Listen."

And together they were going to hold very still and perceive the planet and all of its slightly ensouled objects for the first time. This is a new memory, a joined trajectory, the little planet would concur, far from understanding, but pleased to sense the weight and the attention of the humans and their slightly radiant objects on its surface.

Anna Ziegelhof is a horror and science fiction writer and translator, originally from Germany, now living in the San Francisco Bay Area. She most enjoys philosophical stories with sparks of hope and whimsy and themes such as identity, memory, and belonging. Her short fiction can be found, among others, in *The Horror Library, Luna Station, Solarpunk Magazine, The Future Fire, Daily Science Fiction,* and Flametree Press. Her literary translation work has been featured in Dark Moon Books' *Fantasmagoriana Deluxe.* Anna is an academic with a subject background in Sociology and Jewish Studies. She is also a language-nerd and has worked as a language instructor, editor, and linguist in the tech industry. When she isn't writing she enjoys encountering strange places, being in nature, and looking at art. Online she can be found at www.annaziegelhof.com and occasionally on Instagram as @annawithaz

# The Scholar's Claim

by Michael Vance


**D**ate: 14th day of the Season of the Flowers, 863rd year of the New Era
Discovery


*I am Earick al'Avron, leader of the Galeas expedition. The others look
to me.*

*I cannot let them know that we are lost.*

Footsteps approached, then stopped a few feet away, and Earick
smiled. Staring down at the decaying map, he slowly moved to gather his
precious papers.

"The others are growing impatient?" he asked, half-turning his head.

"The sun is almost up." His son, Adriel, stepped into the clearing
behind, his eyes also fixed on the papers strewn on the forest floor.
Imagining the questions that were coming, Earick said, "Here, you carry
these. They're important." The boy's eyes widened, and when Earick
nodded, Adriel knelt to collect the maps and his father's written notes.
*No, not a boy any longer,* Earick thought, watching him. *Twenty-five
years old and a man, now. I wish his mother could have seen him.*

There was something in the way the lad moved, a hesitation that drew
the moment out unnecessarily.

"Ask," Earick said, trying to sound patient, and drawing another look
of surprise from his son. "Is it the others? You've heard them muttering
that we are lost, am I correct? That I have landed the Galeas in the wrong
place, and this trek inland will lead us all to death?"

Adriel surprised Earick by laughing. The sound filled the small

clearing, and Earick blinked, trying to wave away a cloud of insects.

"Nothing as dramatic as that, Father, though they are worried. Can you blame them, after three weeks in this—" He broke off with a gesture that took in the canopy overhead, and seemed to indicate much else. Then his eyes became serious. "Although, you saying that does make me wonder what you were thinking, just now."

Placing a hand to the eagle pendant around his neck, Earick said a silent prayer asking for guidance. For wisdom.

"Certainly not that the expedition is lost," he lied. "Come along. It is your job to gather the Merak'i—" He broke off, sensing something in the boy.

"There is a problem with the Merak'i" Adriel said reluctantly. "Something new. They don't seem to want to go further inland – I believe they are afraid of something. Terrified, in fact. I'm not certain I can force them onward."

Earick nodded, thinking. They had met the strange creatures seventeen days ago, one day after leaving the Greatship Galeas at anchor in a strange bay. At first both sides had cautiously retreated, but then the Merak'i had come hopping into the open, evidently curious, and the crew of the expedition had attempted to communicate with them by means of gestures and hand signals. There had been some debate amongst the crew about whether the creatures were sentient or mere beasts, and more than one member of the team had noted their resemblance to oversized rodents. They had been ready to give up and move on when Adriel had displayed some worthless trinkets to the creatures. Their gabbling had stopped immediately, and they gathered hungrily, sniffing at the small stones, the bits of ribbon, and eventually a deal of sorts had been struck. Now the Merak'i accompanied them inland, and despite Earick's initial disapproval, he had to admit that their assistance had been invaluable.

"Offer them whatever we have left," Earick said, and together they started off through the trees, Adriel falling into step beside Earick.

"We caught some of them rooting through one of the packs," Adriel said slowly, a small frown on his face. "Some of the others don't trust them now – they think they are more intelligent than what they have let on and mean to rob us blind. Or, worse, leave us out here."

Earick chuckled, suddenly grateful for this short time alone with his son.

"They're simple things," he said. "Curious. Also, harmless. And they know this jungle. And quite frankly, we need them now. Besides that," he added, "I have seen the way that young girl, Larayne, looks at you when you are working with them. She seems impressed."

Adriel blushed at the mention of the girl, but not the way he would have a few years earlier. A silent look was exchanged between father and son, and as they moved forward again both men wore thoughtful expressions.

"Father," Adriel said finally, as they forced their way through thick jungle, guided by the agitated calls of the Merak'i in the distance. "What is going to happen to us here?"

They both stopped. Flies swarmed, and shafts of sunlight cast through gaps in the canopy caused the air to dance between them.

"I have told you the stories since you were a boy, Adriel, a thousand times—"

"Told to a boy," Adriel cut in. "Do you see a child here?"

"You know," Earick replied slowly. "When I was a fresh-faced lad just out of the university, I made a pilgrimage up to Savonne. There is a skeleton there – one of the Adelphi, they claimed – that was dug up somewhere and brought to the museum in Savonne. Some of the bones were missing, but visitors are allowed to enter and see the skeleton – all pieced back together and over seven feet tall. It was nothing human, and though it was a thousand years dead I swear I could feel it staring back at me. I have known since that day that they were real, and that my destiny is to find them. I have trekked the known world since then, searching. Humanity grows, Adriel, and as we stretch our hand out over the horizon, someday we will find their lost city. *I* will find it. They are *here*. I am certain."

*Please God, let us not be lost.*

"Angels from the heavens," Adriel mused. "Who leave their skeletons behind."

They walked again, until they rejoined the rest of the expedition, and there was a sudden hush at their appearance. Earick noted the expectant faces as the tired expedition rose to its collective feet and knew that they still trusted him.

He led them onward.

Deeper. Ever deeper, because there was only forward now.

At noon, there was a cry from up ahead, and the party staggered into sunlight, the Merak'i falling into sudden silence. Earick's breath caught as he saw it, laid out in a valley below, all stony spires and moss-draped towers. He muttered a prayer, and around him, some of the others fell to their knees weeping. Sunlight glinted off what looked like gold atop one of the towers. Of the Adelphi, the gods themselves, there was no sign. But that meant nothing, he told himself, his eyes sweeping the strange ruins. Because they had found it.

Erebos, the lost city of the gods.

Down in the tombs, Adriel was waiting. He had something to show his father, he had said, something important.

Images of the Adelphi decorated the walls of the burial chamber, their strange forms captured in a thousand different activities. In the centre of the chamber, a stone statue knelt at the head of a sarcophagus, head down, shouldering a staff of some kind. The sarcophagus, of course, was empty, but Earick recognised the form of the statue from the museum in Savonne. In the past months, they had found no sign of the actual Adelphi, living or dead, but they knew for certain now that this place had once been their home.

"Father." It was the young woman, Larayne, who spoke. Straightening from where she had been studying the strange Adelphi wall paintings, she smiled as she approached him. At some point she had started calling him 'father', and he nodded at her now, liking her, but his eyes were on his son.

"I wasn't sure you would come," Adriel said. "I told Larayne we had slim odds of getting you away from the books."

Earick shifted uncomfortably, unsure if he was being chided. But Adriel was right. Though the city stood aged and empty, one thing had been found in abundance: books. Entire libraries of them, with shelves lined up dusty and ancient as if waiting to be found. "The object you found last week, Adriel – I believe it is a translation device, some kind of grammar, or a key to their language. I want to show it to you—"

"Good!" Adriel looked sharply at Larayne, and they shared a look. "That's what I wanted to talk to you about, in a way. The books, the libraries – understanding all this. Come and look, father." He reached out and took Earick's arm and guided him over to one wall of the chamber. "All of the tombs we have found so far have one thing in common, and that is that they all depict the libraries in some form or other. We see the Adelphi building them, we see them writing their books – but I don't think that the libraries *were* libraries." He broke off, staring at the wall, his gaze moving rapidly across the painted images.

"Look here – this woman is clearly writing in a book. And here they are carrying the book somewhere—"

"Merak'i?" Earick interrupted, looking more closely. The images were worn by time, but it was not the woman carrying the book, he could see. Rather she was leading two Merak'i, who between them carried a book.

"Yes, yes," Adriel said impatiently. "They were slaves, it seems, or servants to the Adelphi, but they were certainly here that far back, and living in the city. And look where they take the book. What we have been calling a library. There are books there but look what she does." The Adelphi woman seemed to be kneeling over the book. Her eyes were closed, and she held the book to her face so that her lips touched it.

"This appears elsewhere," Adriel continued. "Look what happens to her next."

The Adelphi woman lay flat, and something seemed to be emerging from her chest.

"She died?" Earick asked, wondering if this was her tomb. He shivered.

"Possibly," Adriel said, in a tone that clearly said he did not believe that to be the case. "The spirit leaving the body through her chest – it could be. So, she wrote a book, and died in a library for some reason? No, I believe this was a ritual, something religious, and the book was destroyed but not the woman."

"So, they... sacrificed... the books?" Earick was struggling to understand, but Adriel nodded with excitement at this.

"That's what I believe. The books were *consumed* somehow when they were destroyed. And I think I know a way to test it."

Earick felt his heart stutter. "Test this? How?"

Adriel's face became guarded, and Earick saw Larayne wrap her fingers around his arm as if supporting him.

"You won't like it, father. It will damage some of the books. Only a few pages, but they would be lost forever."

"Absolutely not." Afterwards, he would realise that he had not meant it to sound so harsh, so final. But in that moment, it echoed through the chamber like a scream. "We have risked our lives, Adriel – *all* of us have – to find this place. Nothing here can be destroyed. Look around you, at what has been lost already."

Breathing heavily, Earick pushed himself away from the wall. *My only son.* Nothing could be allowed to come between them.

Nothing.

"God help me," he said. "Destroy them how?"

Adriel met his eyes with a steady gaze. "Fire," he said. "I mean to burn them."

A vast, silent moment stretched out between them. Finally, Earick turned away, and with heavy steps retraced his path out of the tomb. *Did I just agree?* he wondered. *I would do anything not to lose the boy. Absolutely anything. Allow the entire city to burn down...*

Stumbling, he made his way upward into Erebos. People spoke to him as he passed, but he brushed them off and hurried for home. *Must think.*

On the table in his bedroom was the odd, cylindrical device Adriel had brought to him the week before. Made of ivory, it appeared to be a portion of a gigantic tusk, taken from a creature of some kind. It was as thick as Earick's arm and almost as long and was inscribed along its length with thousands of strange symbols. A smooth gold sleeve banded one end, the sleeve also cut with a thousand different symbols, and when you moved the sleeve down the tusk new symbols were formed by the combinations.

It was their writing, the key to the Adelphi language – he was sure of it as he pushed the thing aside bitterly. Because it was also useless to him. It would take a hundred years for him to understand the letters, to see how to combine them properly, and then use them to actually read one of the Adelphi's ancient books.

Lovingly, he lifted a book from the table, held it to his face the way the woman in the tomb painting had done. Who would make a book, only to destroy it?

*We know nothing of them.*

Gently, he opened the book and ran his hand over the soft pages, admiring the strange, beautiful writing. As the pages folded gently under his fingers a small imperfection caught his eye. The book seemed to open unnaturally near the middle and turning to the spot he found two damaged pages there. No, not damaged. Torn.

Furious, he cursed aloud. Furtive footsteps sounded behind him, drawn by his shout, and from the corner of his eye, he saw two Merak'i enter the room and cower in the doorway. He could feel their eyes on him. On the book.

Years later, he would recall his initial instinct. *Hide it.* He had an idea who had taken the pages, of course. Soon, others would know.

Working quickly, he wedged the book open, and worked the two pages gently, trying not to tear them further. There could be no trace left.

*Tear them out by the roots.*

The Merak'i had entered the room now, were watching him, but he ignored them, and frantically separated the damaged pages from the rest of the book. Finally, almost sobbing, he crumpled what was left of the torn pages in his fist and hurled them to the floor. Then he collapsed into a chair, cradling the book, and trying to think.

It was only much later when he rose and set the book gently down on the table again, that he noticed that the crumpled pages were nowhere to be found.

Date: 7th day of the Season of the Sun, 873rd year of the New Era

There was no time left. Already Erebos felt empty, and Earick prayed the Galeas would still be waiting for him when he returned.

*He is my son. No matter what else has happened, he is still my son.*

It was the Merak'i he noticed first before he arrived at the great library. A dozen of them gathered before the doors, and it struck him how they resembled a guard of some sort. Despite himself, he felt his feet slowing as they turned to face him, their quiet chatter suddenly silenced. One of them, he saw, held a staff, and seemed to lean on it for support. In his mind, Earick saw a spear. They watched him with wide eyes as he approached.

*So unlike the creatures we found, so many years ago. They have changed. But why? How?*

We have changed too, he admitted to himself, feeling sick.

The Merak'i separated before him, opening a path to the door, and he nodded his head in thanks as he passed. Somehow, they were creatures no longer, and they themselves seemed to realise that now. They had built homes around the library at some point; simple dwellings, but there were a dozen of the small domes huddled together there now. Earick saw the young ones playing in the small yards. There were human children among them, he noted. Perhaps Lena...

He found his son slumped in one of the small chambers that lined the perimeter of the library, his head sagging, and his eyes wide open and staring. Before him sat one of the Adelphi's bowls – small, white, and made of a substance that seemed indestructible. Prayer bowls, Adriel called them. There was ash in the bowl, Earick saw. Walking over he reached down and rubbed his fingers in it, finding a few small scraps of paper still intact. Distantly he noted the writing, but turned away quickly, his throat aching. That battle had been lost long ago.

Urgently he shook his son by the shoulder, wondering if today might be the day he did not awaken. But slowly the grey eyes focused, the shallow breathing quickened. He was still seeing that other world, Earick knew, but there was so little time now. He had to hurry. He would carry the boy from here, if necessary.

"Father." It broke his heart to hear the word. "You need to go, father, they won't wait."

Startled, Earick crouched down. "Who, Adriel?" Was he still in the dream?

"The others. Aboard the Galeas."

So. He knew.

"Calvin is holding the Greatship, Adriel. He will wait for me to return, with you, and Larayne and Lena. Where are they, Adriel?"

Adriel's eyes drifted.

"Father, before you go. Promise me that you will not take any of the books. You must promise me. Because if you do, the others will know, and they will kill you for the books. I can't stop them."

Earick swallowed, and looked around, his skin prickling. Outside the chamber, people wandered like ghosts.

Adriel reached up and grabbed him with sudden, surprising strength. "Promise, Father. I want you to get away safely. Please."

Feeling tears starting, Earick eased his son down gently.

"We have no books, Adriel. We argued about that, you can imagine, but I forbade it, and for once the others listened. We took some things, but none of the books." He laughed suddenly, but stopped short when he heard the awful sound it made. "I have the translating device, though I won't need it now. Maybe I can learn how it works, when we arrive home." *If* we make it home, he reminded himself silently. "We can't risk the books leaving these shores, Adriel, even to learn what knowledge they might contain. Not now that we have seen what they can do, what they really are. So, we will leave empty-handed. What you are doing here, Adriel – I believe it is what destroyed the Adelphi themselves. It will destroy you, too, and everyone who stays. Where is Larayne? And your daughter. We can find them and take them both."

"Larayne didn't want to see you," Adriel mumbled, his eyes beginning to close. "And Lena stays. Because *I* stay. I'm not sure where she is just now…"

Earick wanted to see Lena, one last time. He had contemplated taking her, no matter what his son said. Instead, he reached up, removed the eagle pendant from around his neck, and placed it in Adriel's limp hand. Then he gently closed the fingers. Feeling ancient, he stood and stared down at his son one last time, unashamed by the tears now streaming down his face.

As he stood there one of the Merak'i eased noiselessly into the room and stepped around him. When Earick left, the Merak'i placed its face gently into the prayer bowl, seeming to search for something.

He was Adriel al'Earick, and he was, he supposed, the leader of his people now, though few remained. More than half had left with his father, and every day now others were lost to the strange dream of the ancient city. Those who remained had lost the ability to care for themselves, and if not for the loyal Merak'i, Adriel knew they would all have died by now.

"Near dark," his companion, Finn, said. "We should return, Adriel. We are finding nothing, tonight." A pair of Merak'i had been sniffing around the walls behind Finn, and they stood now as if to listen. *Are they here to aid us, or are they shepherds?* Adriel thought, watching them. They stared back silently with intelligent eyes. *They want us to find the books, he thought. Because, like us, they need the books now, and we are better at the finding than they are. Still, one thing we are better at than them.*

"What if there are no more?" Finn said suddenly, startling him.

"Books?" He could *feel* the Merak'i, directly behind them, listening. "There are thousands more, Finn. You've seen the city – how it was. When they were here. More will be found."

"I'm not so sure anymore," Finn said quietly, pointing. "Look at our people, how they search now." Three men and a woman wandered a field beside them, gazing sightlessly around. "Those four were there yesterday when we passed. The books won't be found lying in a field, Adriel. Pray that the Merak'i hunters have better luck."

*Will they share what we need?* Adriel wondered silently. *What happens when we are no longer capable of searching at all?*

There were small packs of Merak'i out looking even now. He could hear their distant cries, the calls from one camp to the other. They dug on their own; he had seen their excavations and their teams ranging out around Erebos. So organised. They had fashioned tools as well, that they used to dig and search the ruins of Erebos. Was it habit, he wondered. Had they effectively been trained for this, after years with the people of the Galeas expedition? Or did they search for their own purposes now, for themselves?

The sun was setting over Erebos, and something in the misty beauty of the light slanting over the towers skewered him, froze him, and he thought he smelled smoke. Terror filled him, and for an instant, he knew what was about to happen. He watched from afar as his foot moved forward, and he stepped down—

*And he was Aiyana, of the House of Haseya. The rising sun against the bone-white towers caught his eye, and his steps slowed, and he felt something move within his mind where the ancestors lived. But this was not them, speaking to him out of time – it was something else, and he knew that some other presence had found him. Only this one was wrong, somehow. Twisted. Tainted. Not Adelphi. And he could feel it looking out through his eyes, and he thought of his own great book that he was yet to write and knew that something from the future had found him today.*

*The Merak'i? Could it be?*

*He looked around, his wide, oval eyes quickly finding a pair nearby. There were always Merak'i nearby, though soon, he knew, that would not be the case. For these beasts of burden had violated the holy places, had desecrated the sacred books they had been set to care for. It was an abomination, a sacrilege, a sin for which there could be no forgiveness, and Aiyana made a sign angrily. Like animals, they had chewed the great tomes, and ingested the words of the Adelphi ancestors. And in doing so had permanently broken the perfect chain of memory that went back in time to when the first Adelphi learned to Inscribe the books, and so pass his life, and his memories, on to all who would come after. And in doing so, live forever.*

*No longer. For the first time in millennia, some had been lost, and now retribution must follow. As Aiyana imagined it, the mind of the Adelphi whispered to him, all those voices in his head from ages past, and he saw what would happen.*

*A purge. A culling. For even in the Merak'i the pages still lived, and that could never be permitted. In his mind, Aiyana could see it – the Adelphi warriors resplendent in their armour and glowing in the sun, as they set to the slaughter. The streets would run with Merak'i blood, and their numbers would be decimated, until only a few were left and allowed to live. Those would be exiled from Erebos, and forever cursed with the memory of what had happened, so they would never forget.*

*Never again would they dare set foot in the great city of the Adelphi. Forever after they would live as animals, and nothing more.*

*Until the others came.*

*That other voice, speaking to him now. The future opened to his eye.*

*Strange beings would wander the city, and in his thoughts, he could see them. Not Adelphi, and not the Merak'i, either. They would come from afar, and in imitation of the Adelphi they would burn the books. Drunk on the visions in the smoke, they would consume all of the books, until none were left, and the great Libraries were gone. And then the Adelphi would end, the People extinguished forever.*

*But retribution would follow, as it must. And through his grief, Aiyana saw that though the newcomers destroyed the books, so in turn would the books destroy the newcomers. Their minds would wither and rot, overwhelmed and destroyed by the visions, until eventually, they would wander Erebos as no more than ghosts. Ghosts in a city already haunted.*

*But we will be gone.*

*This could not be. Retribution was not enough; not for this. These ones should be cursed with memory, like the Merak'i, so that the world would know what they had done to the Adelphi. Know, and never forget.*

*No. Retribution was not enough...*

—Into a world that was decayed, and empty, with the sun sinking low on a place that felt like a memory. Adriel staggered forward, not understanding where he was – who he was – and looking around he found himself alone and night falling. How long had he stood there, he wondered, lost in that other time? Had it been real?

Yes. Confused and shattered, he made for home, feeling a new idea growing inside his mind.

The Merak'i had constructed a small settlement outside the building where Adriel and Larayne made their home. Two dozen domed dwellings clustered there, and the Merak'i strode purposefully about as Adriel passed. He nodded to one of the Merak'i, who stood outside a small wooden fence. There was an orchard on the other side of the fence, one of the strange and beautiful groves that grew only where the Merak'i lived. Or where they died. They were graveyards, supposedly, where the Merak'i dead were buried. No one knew for sure. These were not the small rodent-like creatures from the vision any longer.

*It has accelerated their evolution,* he realised. *Growing them into something more than they were, while we were destroyed.*

Silently he passed into his house, called for Lena. He could hear Larayne moving about, but she ignored him, and he heard a door close. He continued: it was not Larayne he was looking for. She had quit the Adelphi books when Lena turned five, and they realised that their daughter had been affected by the books without ever having burned one of the pages. Her eyes had given it away, and her eerie, constant silence, as if she did not live in this world at all. They had recognised it immediately, and had hardly spoken in the years since, knowing they were both to blame.

Ghosts.

We are ghosts already. I cannot let that happen. They wanted to curse us with memory, but I will not let it be a curse. I will not be forgotten – Lena, my father – I will not allow them to be forgotten. I have seen how the Adelphi wrote the books, the strange ritual by which life was passed to the pages, so it could live again in others. I know how it was done – and how we can do it, too. Yes, we will write our own stories, and we will live on, and someday someone will remember. Somebody must remember us.

Entering his study, at first, he did not see her there, huddled low beside the small table. Lena was a small child, and when she turned her head now her eyes held no surprise at being discovered. She did not smile, or rise, merely blinked, and moved a small wooden box from her lap to the table. His heart hammering, Adriel saw that the box was open. His precious, secret box. Slowly he walked forward, unspeaking, looking from Lena to the box.

Inside the box were perhaps a dozen tattered scraps of paper. He had been months scrounging them – from the ashy remains of the prayer bowls, or old books long thought depleted, and even from the homes of the other settlers while they were out wandering. A king's ransom, he thought, gathering the lot of them up in one hand and then letting them flutter back into the box like gemstones. Hoarded against a time when there were no more books to be found in the city. When the last of them had been dug out and burned in the last prayer bowl, and there were no more.

Hoarded against the end of the world.

Half of them were missing. There was no need to count them, to lay them out, and learn by the shapes and symbols remaining just which ones were gone. Sickness punched through his gut, both at the loss, and the certainty at who had taken them.

Lena. His baby.

Unable to look at her, shattered by guilt, he closed the box and gripped it in a shaking fist. It had to be destroyed. Buried. Lost – far away from here. And Lena might be found again – in memory. Not lost, this little ghost. This price was simply too high.

"I'm sorry," he said finally, in a trembling, pathetic voice. Still, he could not look at her, and in a sudden rage, he turned and hurled the box against the wall, then staggered toward his daughter. He intended to sweep her up in his arms and leave, but when he reached her, he collapsed instead, crushing her small body to his chest. "I'm sorry." He felt his tears soaking into her hair.

Unseen, a single Merak'i entered the room, a large male. It watched them for a short time, and then turned its attention to the broken box on the floor, the scattered bits of ancient paper. The Merak'i cocked its head to one side, considering, then lowered its head to sniff the scraps of paper. The smell was wrong – the burnt edges tainting the paper. But there were words there – *pieces* of words, at least.

Lowering its head, the Merak'i began to feed.


Date: 28th day of the Season of Winds, 912th year of the New Era

Discovery


The city was quiet in an unnatural way, and it made Flinn's skin crawl.

They had clawed their way up the coast through the jungle for weeks, before finding Erebos. Now, Flinn stared in wonder at the enormous structures, tears shining in his eyes. The legends were true, the stories of the lost Galeas expedition, and the city of the gods – it was true.

Strange figures – not human – were working on some of the buildings; he could hear hammer blows coming from above. They might have been animals, but for the way they moved, and the way they chattered as they gathered to watch the newcomers. He saw intelligence in their dark eyes.

"Move slowly," Flinn told his team. "Keep your hands visible to them, and let me speak."

Were these the Adelphi, he wondered. The gods themselves? What would he say to them?

They continued, toward the centre of the city, until they reached a large domed structure, surrounded by smaller buildings and huge flowering trees. There were people there, he was shocked to see; humans. Men and women, some working at various tasks, and some simply wandering. Flinn saw a woman his own age and approached her.

There was something about her eyes that disturbed him, and he took an involuntary step backwards before stopping himself. She seemed to stare right through him, and he knew she was not seeing him even when she stood directly in front of him.

Flinn spoke, telling the woman how far he had come in search of this place. She said nothing when he finished, and he knew she had not heard him. What was wrong with her? Behind him, the crew muttered uneasily, and he willed them to silence.

Then one of the creatures gathered there spoke, a quick series of clicks and soft sounds directed at the woman, and she turned her head slightly. When she did not move, the creature spoke again, gently, and this time she waved a hand toward the building behind her and began to walk.

"You lot wait here for me," Flinn said. "Don't follow unless I call."

"Flinn," his wife, Miriam, said. "There is something wrong here—"

"I know. So, wait. And be ready."

Alone he followed the strange woman into the building. Once inside, he looked around at wooden shelves lined with books. A class seemed to be in session in the middle of the room, with both humans and the strange creatures seated in a circle around the room. Many of them, he saw, were children, and all of them held books open on their laps. His guide stared sightlessly down at the children, and Flinn stepped forward, looking over her shoulder. What he saw made his heart hammer.

The writing, the strange shapes the child was making – he had seen it before. Back at the ship he had a device – a sort of tusk, acquired at great cost – with letters like this carved into it. Thousands of these same letters. He had to return to retrieve the device, and decipher—

The creature at the head of the circle spoke to the child. The boy looked up, and Flinn stared down into serene grey eyes, and saw the eagle pendant around the boy's neck.

Then the boy reached down and gently tore a page from the book and handed it to Flinn wordlessly. Shaking, Flinn accepted it, wondering what he should say. But the creature spoke again, this time to the woman who had guided Flinn into the room, and slowly she seemed to waken from a trance. Her eyes travelled the room without seeing it, and she beckoned Flinn to follow, then began to walk. Flinn's eyes met those of the strange creature, and he was certain he saw disapproval there – or was it sorrow – but he knew he was meant to follow the woman.

They entered a small chamber, with a white bowl at its centre, and the woman sat. Flinn sat across from her. Something was glowing in the base of the bowl, he saw, a pale cube that emanated warmth though it was very small. Wordlessly the woman took the page that the child had handed her and placed it into the bowl, and when the page touched the cube, it rippled into flame.

The woman dipped her head over the bowl and closed her eyes, and he saw her breathe deeply. Straightening, she seemed to see him at last and reached up one cold hand to the back of his neck, and Flinn realised she wanted him to inhale the smoke as well. It was some sort of ritual. Understanding, he lowered his face over the bowl and—

*He was Earick al'Avron, leader of the Galeas expedition, and he stood on the deck of the Greatship with his son Adriel at his side. Before them the sea was calm and flat, glowing blue and green and glittering in the afternoon sun. Dolphins had found them and bounded alongside the ship. There were sea birds overhead, and Earick knew that land was close.*

*They had travelled for months, for years. Through storms, and sickness, and starvation. For this. He could feel it, coming closer, and he reached over suddenly to grab Adriel's shoulder. His son looked at him, his eyes shining, and Earick hugged him close, laughing, loving the boy.*

*Overhead, someone shouted, and it was picked up all across the Galeas. Somewhere, up ahead, land had been sighted.*

Michael Vance is a resident of Ontario, Canada. His short fiction has previously appeared in *On Spec*, the *Tesseracts* anthology, and most recently in *Black Sheep* magazine. He is currently hard at work raising his twelve year old son, who is also a published author.

# Birds of a Feather

by Sarina Dorie

When Maggie's son, Charlie, insisted he was a bird, and would only eat nuts and seeds, she hoped it was only a phase. Her older sister told her this was common for seven-year-olds; her daughter would only eat hot dogs. After two weeks of this diet, Charlie's poop came out white and liquid like a bird's. Though Maggie's husband seemed unconcerned, she took him to the doctor anyway.

Dr. Bensen's weathered face crinkled into amusement as he laughed. "Maybe if you ate seeds for two weeks, the same thing would happen to you. See if you can get him to eat some bugs, they'll be good protein for his diet."

Maggie left in disgust.

Two days later, when Maggie went to call Charlie in for dinner, she found him on the roof. He wore what looked like a pair of fake wings over his shirt. The feathers glistened with hues of blue and green like his raven hair. With the setting sun behind him and the autumn wind tousling his hair, he resembled some kind of Greek god more than her child. Maggie's momentary awe turned to maternal instinct when he stepped toward the edge of the roof.

"Oh, no you don't! Get down from there this instant!" she shouted.

"Okay," he said, bending his knees and preparing to jump.

Her heart thundered with trepidation. "No! You get down the way you got up. I will not have you breaking your neck trying to fly off the roof."

He rolled his eyes. "I won't break my neck. Even if I do fall, I made myself a cushion." He pointed to the pile of red and brown leaves he'd raked into a heap.

Maggie gave him her sternest I'm-your-mother-and-you-will-listen-to-me look. Charlie trudged over to the oak tree next to the roof and shimmied himself down. Maggie tried to spot him the entire time in case he fell.

As he was climbing down, Maggie noticed the tear in the back of his shirt to accommodate the wings. She yanked the fabric down a little further, expecting to see straps under his arms, but there were none. She pulled at one of the black wings, surprised by its warmth.

"Ow! Mom, that hurts!"

They seemed to be fastened to his back.

"Did you superglue this to your skin? Who helped you?"

He hopped down from the tree, trying to squirm away. "No, they grew there overnight. Dad said it isn't anything to be worried about."

"What?" Her voice grew shrill and sharp. "You went to school like this?"

"It's okay. I wore my book bag all day. Dad said it was fine."

She inspected the wings carefully, noticing the way his skin blended into feathery down and then continued into longer feathers. She hefted him under one arm and kicked toys out of her path as she carried him into the garage.

He was as light as a bird with hollow bones. That diet of birdseed had to be making him malnourished.

Fred sat at his cluttered workbench, unbothered by the mound of broken electronics and half-finished projects. In the heart of this mess, he glued what looked like a miniature house together. It was blue like their house.

Glasses perched on his prominent nose, his profile looked more hawk-like than usual. He didn't glance up from his glueing. "I'll be right there. I just need another minute."

Maggie stopped next to him, waiting until he met her eyes. "This is from your side of the family, isn't it? What have you been hiding from me?"

Fred instantly hunched over. "I don't know what you're talking about." He returned to glueing.

She snatched away the wooden house and plopped Charlie into his lap. "Do you see those wings? Charlie said you allowed him to go to school like that. Is that correct?"

Charlie launched himself off his father's lap, looking at his father pleadingly.

Fred squirmed under her gaze. "That's correct. But it's all right. No one saw. I told Charlie to hide them."

Maggie couldn't believe her ears. He was completely missing the point. "Are those things real? Where did they come from?"

"Hey, you're the one who's adopted. Maybe you're part harpy." He winked at her, then reached for the house in her hands. There was a hole and a peg on one side. Maggie set the birdhouse on a disassembled toaster out of his reach.

Fred sighed, setting down his tube of glue. He smoothed his fingers over Charlie's black wings, the colour not so different from his own hair. When he finally spoke, his voice was almost a whisper. "I'd hoped it would skip a generation."

Maggie stared at his earnest expression, unable to believe her ears. "You'd hoped *what* would skip a generation?"

"There are some things about my family I haven't told you." He rubbed his nose self-consciously. "Our son is a bird man, well, bird boy. He's sort of like a lycanthrope, only he'll change into a bird."

Maggie shook her head, unable to believe what he was saying. "How do you stop it? Is there a cure? Some kind of medicine?"

"No. Really, hon, it's not that bad. I mean, sure it would be more convenient not to turn into a bird every once in a while, but I've managed to hide it pretty well."

She stared at him, too stunned to say anything else.

"You kept this from me?" Tears filled her eyes.

"When we were dating, I thought you knew and that was why you found me so rakishly handsome. Then when I realised you didn't know...I was going to tell you before we married. Then I was going to wait until our first anniversary. Then I thought I should wait until after Charlie was born." He sighed despondently. "I just didn't want this to ruin things between us."

Maggie was so angry she was shaking. "You lied to me for all these years, and you didn't expect that to ruin things between us?"

"I never lied. I just never showed you my true self." Fred didn't meet her eyes.

This was worse than if Fred had concealed having an STD before they'd married and then passed it on to her and Charlie. At least if she could have contracted being a bird too – she'd be part of this. She could have commiserated with her husband and son. But instead, Fred had hidden the truth from her for years. She didn't know what was worse, that he was something strange and otherworldly, or that he'd chosen to shut her out. Her spirits sank with her inability to change the situation.

Charlie sprang toward the door. "Now can I go back up to the roof and jump off?"

"No," Maggie said firmly. "And put a coat on if you go outside."

Needing someone to confide in, Maggie locked herself in the bathroom and dialled her sister's number on the cordless phone.

"Mags, what's wrong?" Gwynne said.

At the sound of her sister's voice, her words turned into a blubbery mess. "My son is turning into a bird! And my husband knew this would happen. He's some kind of were-bird, and he's kept it a secret."

"What? Did you just say Fred is a bird?"

"Yes," Maggie wailed. "And he never told me." She blew her nose. For a long moment, the crackle of phone static was all Maggie could hear.

Gywnne's voice was the calm she needed in this emotional storm. "He might not have lied to you. Remember when you and Fred were dating, and he kept joking he was 'cuckoo for you'?"

Maggie closed the lid of the toilet seat and sat down. "Yeah. So?"

"And another time, you told me Fred said something like, 'Cuddling is for the birds. It's a good thing for you that I'm a bird.' Maybe he wasn't joking. Have you considered he was trying to tell you and gauge how you'd react?"

Maggie had forgotten all about the 'cuddling is for the birds.' Fred did have a lot of other bird sayings. "There was that first time I invited him to go Christmas carolling with the family, and Mom asked him how he got to be such a good whistler. He told her it was because he was a bird." And there was that one time he told her could fly...

Every time he'd said things like that, she'd giggled or rolled her eyes.

Maybe he'd thought she was laughing at him. She'd thought his hints were jokes, and he had never shared the truth with her or shown her his wings – if he had wings. She'd never seen them.

She wiped her eyes and sniffled. Even knowing he'd tried to tell her, didn't make her feel better. She still felt... alone.

"I feel like I've been told I was adopted all over again."

"I'm sorry," Gwynne said, her voice cracking.


Maggie remembered the exact moment she'd found out she'd been adopted. She had been six. She'd been playing with dolls with Gwynne when they'd started arguing over a toy. Maggie snatched it up.

There was venom in her older sister's countenance. "Yeah, well, you know what? You're adopted. Mom didn't even want you, but a stork dropped you on our doorstep, so we had to take you in."

Tears burned Maggie's eyes as she ran to her mother who was preparing a dinner salad in the kitchen. She sprinkled raisins on Gwynne's salad since she liked them special, and sunflower seeds on Maggie's because that was her favourite.

"Mommy! Gwynne said I'm adopted! She said you don't – didn't—" From the stricken look on her mother's face, she saw it was true. Maggie covered her eyes and sobbed.

Her mother left dinner and drew Maggie into her arms. "Oh, honey. I'm so sorry this was the way you found out. Your father and I decided we wouldn't tell you about being adopted until you were older. But just because a stork left you on our doorstep doesn't mean we don't want you."

"A stork? Like in the book you used to read to me at night?" Only being six, and not understanding the workings of where babies came from, a stork seemed an adequate explanation. On the other hand, there was that neighbour lady with the huge belly who had six children. Her daughter, Sarah, said they kept popping out of her belly. That seemed way more complicated than the stork. "Not everyone gets a stork baby?"

"That's right. You're special. Your father and I – well, we'd been... I couldn't... You see, there was this baby in my belly and it had something wrong with it, so it... died. I prayed and prayed for another baby. A few days later, as we were just getting out of the car after church, a giant bird flew over our house. It was winter and the sun had set, so it was dark, and I could barely see what it was. Gwynne screamed and I grabbed her and shielded her with my body, thinking it was a giant condor or something... bigger. The bird swooped so close to your father that he ducked and put up his hands to cover his head, but as he did so, the stork dropped you right into his arms. It was a miracle. It was just what we wanted. And you've been our baby ever since."

Maggie wiped the tears from her eyes, feeling a little better.

Her mother went on. "We love you and wanted you to be happy and normal and not have to think about this until you're older. Gwynne shouldn't have told you, but now that you know, it might be for the best."

Gwynne apologised later. Though she sounded sincere, that remark continued to haunt Maggie. From that day on, Maggie noticed she was different from her family. Her sister had their mother's chestnut hair and blue eyes and her father's curls. Maggie's hair was blond and straight. Her eyes were brown. She didn't look like anyone.

"Gwynne gets her tidiness from her father and her love of math from me," her mother would brag to PTA ladies. She didn't say Maggie got anything from them.

When Maggie's mother started to grow round with a baby in her belly, Maggie asked, "Why isn't the stork bringing this baby like it did with me?"

"Not everyone can be special like you," her mother said, ruffling her hair.

When her brother was born, Maggie noticed how her parents doted on the new baby and let Gwynne hold him. When Maggie asked to hold the baby, she was told she was too young and might hurt him. Gwynne shared her teddy bear and her special blanket with him.

"You don't ever let me hold Mr. Fluffy," Maggie complained. "Why do you love the baby more than me? Is it because he wasn't brought by a stork like I was?"

Gwynne sheepishly held the teddy bear out to her. "You're eight now. You have to stop saying you were brought by a stork. People will think you're weird."

Maggie's past haunted her dreams. She had never felt as though she'd fit in with her adoptive family. Now she didn't feel like she fit in with her own husband and son.

She woke the next morning to the sound of cawing birds coming from the kitchen. As she groggily passed the mess of dishes in the sink and made her way to the coffee pot, she stopped mid-stride, seeing two giant ravens sitting at the kitchen table. Her stomach flip-flopped at the sight of the bowls filled with writhing worms before them. The larger bird was the size of her husband. He leaned over a newspaper, a cup of coffee in front of him.

He wasn't using a coaster on the glass table either.

"Good morning, dear," said the big bird in a sing song voice.

"Morning, Mom," said the smaller bird.

Fred hadn't been joking. They really were birds. Her heart sank. Fred bent his beak over his coffee and slurped it down. The cup shifted, grinding into the glass surface beneath it.

Anger flared up in her. She snatched up a cork coaster from the counter and flopped it down on the table. "When we got this table, you agreed you'd use coasters."

The two birds exchanged glances.

"And you will not eat worms from my good bowls. You can use the camping plates for that." She realised this probably wasn't the time to chide her family for eating worms and not using coasters, and momentarily felt guilty for yelling at them.

Fred tilted his head to the side. Charlie giggled, a high-pitched sound in between a chirp and a whistle.

"What?" Maggie asked.

"This morning Dad told me you're a harpy."

Maggie glared at her husband, about to throw a stack of cork coasters at him, but Charlie added, "He said that's why he married you."

In mythology, harpies were filthy, hag-like birds.

"I am not a harpy. I shower. I wash my hair. I clean house." She glanced at the sink full of dirty dishes and the bags of groceries she still hadn't put away from the day before. "I *sometimes* clean house. That doesn't make me a harpy." Weren't harpies usually ravenous? She wasn't ravenous. She was just a little...peckish from not having her coffee and muffin. And just because some kind of bird dropped her on her parent's doorstep...t hen again, what if it hadn't been a stork? What if it had been a harpy?

She shook her head, pushing the thought away. "And I don't nag and scold as much as a harpy." Well, maybe she did. But harpies were always old and ugly. Is that what they thought of her?

Fred nodded his big bird head and extended a wing around her shoulders. "Of course, dear. I'm sorry. I was just trying to make you feel included."

It took a moment for his words to sink in. Her anger softened. Tears filled her eyes. "Really?"

She didn't know if she was relieved or disappointed not to be a bird like him – or a bird different from him. "So, I'm not really... a harpy?" Her throat tightened around the words.

"I'm sorry, hon." His eyes were full of sorrow. "When we first met in that singing class, I thought you might be because of your beautiful voice. You told me you were delivered by a stork, and I observed you do eat more seeds than most people." His eyes twinkled for a moment before turning sombrer. "But if you do have bird lineage, you aren't a shifter like I am. You might be part harpy, but it isn't enough to give you wings. It's probably only a trace amount in your family ancestry."

"Oh." All those times he'd teased her by calling her a harpy, it had been a way to connect with her, and she'd never known.

She let him fold her under his wing, her head resting against the soft down of his chest. Even as a bird, she felt like she fit comfortably against him.

His voice took on the calm sing song of a lullaby. "I know this bird stuff has been hard on you, and it's going to continue to be hard. I don't want you to feel left out. I want us to be able to navigate this as a family."

She stared up into his black eyes. They were still the same round shape as his human eyes. "That's so sweet."

He leaned his beak toward her lips.

She pulled away. "You have worm breath. Don't even think about kissing me until you've brushed your beak."

Charlie half-giggled, half-tweeted at that. "Did you see what Dad made for you?" He swivelled his head toward the window, nearly pecking at the glass as he pointed with his beak.

Maggie gazed out into the yard strewn with autumn leaves. Under the oak tree outside the window, he'd put up a new birdhouse, blue like a miniature version of the house he'd been working on. A family of birds perched on the roof. No, not birds. They weren't moving. Were they wooden?

Fred squirmed next to her, feathery down shifting under her arms. "I, um, carved them myself. Well, mostly carved them."

The biggest bird was black, the smallest bird was identical except for its size. The one between them had a bird body, but it looked like a Barbie head had been stuck on it.

"Harpies are actually more like sirens," he said. "In the most ancient myths, they're known for their beauty and their singing, not their nagging."

She kissed his beak, even if he did have worm breath.

Charlie made a gagging sound. "Eew! Mom! Dad! Do you have to do that in front of me?"

For the first time since this bird situation had begun, Maggie felt like she was part of her family again.

# When the White Peak of Nuraghad Calls Them Home

by Keira Reynolds

Hurmir opened his eyes. White clouds chased each other lazily across a blue sky, momentarily hiding and then revealing the sun. Birds sang and the wind sighed in the trees. The sunlight was warm on his face. His mouth tasted of blood and the air smelled of death.

Something heavy lay across his chest, pinning him to the earth. He tried to push it off, but pain flared as broken bones grated, and his hands were slippery with blood. He managed to lift his head enough to see that it was a dwarven corpse that lay across his chest, one hand still gripping the haft of a battle-axe, the blade buried in the skull of a dead goblin. To his left, corpses lay, dwarf and goblin, clad in battered armour, some still clutching broken weapons, locked together in death. There was blood splashed on dented armour and dead hands and faces, soaking into slashed cloaks and tunics and the trampled earth.

The battle was over then, and either no one had survived, or any who had were too few, and too weak, to tend to the fallen. He had been left for dead. He turned his head to the right, groaning in pain. More corpses, and far off in the distance, the gleaming white snowcapped peak of Nuraghad on the western horizon. Home. He would never see home again.

Close by on his right lay the corpse of a dead goblin in crude leather armour. Probably the sneaky little bastard that had cut him down, stabbing him from behind in the press of battle. He had struck back blindly as he fell and had felt his axe bite. He glared at the corpse. The corpse opened its eyes and glared back.

Hurmir scrabbled for a weapon. His axe was out of sight, buried somewhere under the dead bodies. His dagger was under him, he could

feel the hilt pressing into the small of his back through his chain mail, but trapped and injured as he was, he couldn't reach it. He struggled to push the dead dwarf off him. The goblin had drawn a dagger and raised it high, sunlight flickering on the steel blade as the goblin's hand trembled. With a desperate heave, fighting through the pain, Hurmir managed to roll the dead dwarf aside, but it was far too late now to find a weapon. He threw up his arms in a hopeless attempt to fend off the dagger.

The goblin slammed the blade into the blood-soaked earth between them and fell back with a grunt of pain and exhaustion.

"Why?" Hurmir's throat was dry, and his breathing was shallow, every breath sending pain through his chest. The word came out somewhere between a croak and a gasp. The dagger stood buried hilt-deep in the earth. Could he reach it before the goblin could?

The goblin muttered something guttural and incomprehensible. He stopped, took a breath, and spoke again, this time in the dwarven tongue. "Why bother? You'll be dead soon enough, dwarf." He spat out the word 'dwarf' as though it had a bad taste in his mouth.

"As will you, goblin," Hurmir responded, with much the same emphasis.

"True enough. We'll both be dead soon. Should have stayed in your mountains, dwarf."

"And you shouldn't have raided our farms and villages."

"We wouldn't have, if you hadn't raided ours first."

"Lies. Goblins started the war."

"How do you know? Were you there?"

"Of course not. Dwarves and goblins have been at war since the dawn of days."

"Then who's to say who started it, and what does it matter now anyway?"

"You burned and massacred whole villages. Slaughtered and enslaved the innocent and the helpless. Children, even."

"As did you."

"I have never killed a child." This was true, as far as Hurmir knew. But he remembered goblin villages burning, enraged dwarves cutting down fleeing figures as they ran through the smoke and confusion of battle, with little thought for anything but vengeance.

A long moment passed in which the goblin said nothing.

"Your silence speaks for you, goblin."

"I didn't know." The goblin spoke softly, as much to himself as to Hurmir, staring up into the blue sky as he spoke, his eyes fixed on those white clouds drifting across the blue sky. "A shadow came at me in the chaos of battle, out of the smoke of a burning village. I struck first. My sword stuck in the body and was wrenched from my hand as the shadow fell. I picked up a fallen axe and fought on. After the battle, I looked for my sword. It was a good sword." He shot a bitter glance at Hurmir. "A dead dwarf's sword. I found it buried in the chest of a dead dwarf-child armed with nothing but a length of firewood. I left the sword where it was. I hadn't the heart to wrench it from the body."

"Even a child will take up whatever weapon comes to hand and fight, when he has seen his home burned and his kin slaughtered," said Hurmir, and again he remembered burning goblin villages, and indistinct figures cut down as they ran from the flames.

"Aye." The goblin momentarily turned his head to stare at the dwarf, before looking up again into the blue sky. His voice was barely audible, his expression distant. "Aye. He will."

They were both silent for some time after that. Hurmir watched the white clouds drifting, the warm yellow sun sinking slowly toward the west. "How is it that you speak our language?" he asked.

"You mean how is that a savage, ignorant goblin speaks your oh-so-superior dwarven language?"

"Now that you mention it, that's pretty much what I meant, yes."

"I am... I was... a scout. If you want to know what your enemies are planning, it helps to learn their language. Never met a dwarf who bothered to learn our language, though. I guess no dwarf ever thought we had anything important to say."

The goblin unhitched a waterskin from his belt, fumbling at the leather cord with blood-slick fingers. He raised the skin to his lips, took a long drink, and splashed water on his face, then offered the skin to Hurmir. The dwarf hesitated. The goblin started to laugh, then stopped, the laugh cut off short, wincing in pain.

"It's just water in a goatskin. We don't really make our waterskins out of dwarf skin, or drink dwarf blood, or any of those other silly stories that dwarves tell to frighten their children. Drink or don't drink, dwarf. It makes no difference to me. Just don't make me laugh again or I might have to reconsider my decision not to stab you."

Hurmir took the skin and drank. The water was warm from lying in the sun but otherwise fresh and good.

"You're a very unusual goblin."

"How would you know? How many goblins have you actually talked to? I mean other than yelling *die, goblin, die*, as you ran at them with an axe?"

"You're the first. What's your name?"

"Xaard. Yours?"

"Hurmir."

"Don't expect me to shake your hand, Hurmir, or say I'm happy to meet you."

"Likewise. But I will say that it's better not to die alone."

"Aye. There's that."

Somewhere, not very far away, a wolf howled, a lost, lonely, mournful sound. In the blue sky above, black crows were circling.

"I hope we're both dead before they lose patience," said Hurmir.

"Why do you think I didn't stab you? I might need that dagger later. Wouldn't want it blunted by your armour or jammed between your ribs."

"Is that the only reason?"

"It's what I'm supposed to do. A dying goblin, killing a dwarf with his last breath. They make songs about things like that. Songs to inspire more dying goblins to kill more dying dwarves. Maybe I'm tired of doing what I'm supposed to do."

There was silence again for a time after that, other than an occasional howl from the wolves, the cries of the circling crows, and the sigh of the wind in the grass. Memories drifted by like the white clouds passing overhead. Hurmir's father at work in the fields, guiding the heavy plough behind the oxen, their breath misting in the air, or swinging his hammer in the forge while Hurmir worked the bellows. His mother singing as she spun thread and wove cloth. Thasia lying in his arms, looking up into his eyes and laughing with the dew on her skin and the sunlight in her hair.

He would never see any of them again. They would not even have the consolation of a body to burn.

"Xaard?"

"What?"

"What do goblins believe happens after death?"

"Well, the priests say if you fight well, and kill many dwarves, you go to the great hall, where you eat, drink, and kill more dwarves. But priests lie about many things. They probably lie about that too. What do dwarves believe?"

"Much the same, mostly. Fight well, kill many goblins, go to the great hall under the mountain. But there is a sect called the Khedmulir who believe that we each have a destiny to fulfil. They say if you don't fulfil your destiny in this life, you're reborn to live again in this world, as many times as it takes, until your destiny is fulfilled."

"Gods and goddesses, I hope not. I wouldn't want to live this stinking life again."

"Maybe it doesn't have to be this way, next time."

"Maybe."

Time passed. The sun was warm, the wind was soft and cool, and there was no more pain now. Hurmir remembered dwarves with whom he had grown up, studied, trained, worked in the fields and at the forge, got drunk, marched to war. How many of them had made it back to Nuraghad? How many lay nearby, dead on this blood-soaked field, far from home? Was Xaard thinking similar thoughts?

"Xaard?"

No answer.

"Xaard?"

Still no answer.

The sky was a darker blue now, the white clouds turning to pink and gold. The sun sank toward the mountains in the west, where the white peaks were tinged with crimson. Tomorrow would be a good day.

The wolves howled, closer now, and the crows circled overhead, more of them now, black against the deep blue, circling lower. And then the crows scattered, fleeing in all directions like black, storm-driven leaves. An eagle hung motionless in the sky. It lifted its head, screamed contempt at the crows, and with one majestic beat of its great wings it turned and soared away, westward toward the white peak of Nuraghad.

The crows circled again, and the wolves howled, very close now. Hurmir closed his eyes.

Keira Reynolds is a trans woman, a software developer turned writer. Her stories have appeared in *Luna Station Quarterly* (issue 052) and *A Summer of Sci-Fi and Fantasy* (volume two). She lives in County Kerry, Ireland.

# Rara Avis

by Bruce Boston

While the pale unicorn
hides in the faerie wood,
you fly for the sun
in gold and crimson raiment
to solo the empty sky.

While the fierce griffin
devours the thief,
while the winged dragon
swallows its tail,
you dine on valerian
and cinnamon.

While the fetid breath
of the scaly basilisk
withers shrubs
and splits rocks asunder,
you fashion a nest
for your own cremation.

Of all the magical beasts,
only you, sly phoenix,
can glide the shadow
lands of death
and fish the River Styx.

Only you, mad bird,
go down in fiery plumage
to rise again
from the sizzling marrow
of your bones.

Bruce Boston is the author of sixty books and chapbooks, including the psychedelic coming-of-age novel *Stained Glass Rain* and the dystopian sf novel *The Guardener's Tale*. His poetry and fiction have appeared in hundreds of publications, most visibly in *Amazing, Analog, Asimov's SF, Daily SF, Strange Horizons, Weird Tales, The Nebula Award Anthology* (St. Martins), *Year's Best Fantasy and Horror* (St. Martin's) and *Year's Best Horror* (DAW), and have received numerous awards, most notably, a Pushcart Prize, the Bram Stoker Award, the Asimov's Readers' Award, the Rhysling Dwarf Stars, and Grand Master Awards of the SFPA.

# Alice on Shrooms

by Allen Ashley


Mother showed me the woodland growth
we could cook and eat. warning
that others would give me tummy
ache or crazy dreams.

My head's been addled enough
by the latest events and I already know
that however pretty those red
and white toadstools are –
fly agaric, Mr Dodgson confirms –
one should definitely not consume them.
Leave the polka dot pedestals
for the elves to perch upon.

That caterpillar with his opium
pipe and his words of wisdom...
how long is he intending to sit
on that mushroom? Surely one
day he'll fledge to butterfly
or moth.

I drank some potion, nibbled
here and there. Changed size.
I think my tastebuds won't be
exploring spores or tree-growing fungus
any time soon. A simple jam
sandwich will suffice,
thank you, Nurse.
I won't always be a girl, you
know. I'll live to a senior age
and be lauded in America.
Mr Dodgson would like it there
and appreciate their fungi-fun guy puns
much more than I ever shall.

Allen Ashley is a former President of the British Fantasy Society and is also the founder of the advanced science fiction and fantasy group Clockhouse London Writers. A regular in BFS publications and at BFS events, he has recently been published online at *Sein und Werden, Lothlorien Journal, Green Ink Poetry* and *The World of Myth*. His chapbook *Journey to the Centre of the Onion* – variously described as Slipstream and Atom Punk – was published in hardback and paperback by Eibonvale Press UK in September 2023.

# Lighthouse

by Robin Maginn

I can't stop thinking about the story Gabriel told me before he left. He is full of stories, and this one was about the Four Reds.

About 150 years ago, a troupe of daredevil pilots travelled from quadrant to quadrant performing tricks in formation with their small ships. They'd jettison some kind of active red substance, trailing it behind them as they looped and rolled in unison, creating designs and spectacles like fireworks in slow motion.

They were entertainers. It was probably a fun gig – they would turn up at asteroid mining facilities, or habitational outposts, or deep-spaceports, and just... *show off*. There's so much boredom in space that such show-offs will always engender goodwill. The Four Reds would perform, and then stay over for a few days wherever they were. Quarters and drinks on the house, and they got to live up their legends.

An accident killed all four in one go, mid-performance. A collision that shouldn't have happened and a silent explosion extinguished four lives.

But they're still spotted now and again.

Gabriel claims he saw them once. In the middle of empty space, too far from any refuelling stations for ships that size, he watched vibrant red designs forming and dissipating and reforming for hours.

Now, while I wait for news of Gabriel's return, I look out the window in my room towards a universe that just does not end. No Four Reds out there.

Space is big enough to be full of other ghosts.

The station administrator visited earlier. She held my hand gently as she talked details. So many details. I must admit I found it hard to keep up.

"Have you talked to your family recently?" she asked, as she was leaving.

My attention was elsewhere when she spoke, focussed on another part of my living quarters so I replied, "A few days ago," though, in truth, it has been several weeks. Maybe longer.

The hardest thing to get used to living on this station, living off Earth, isn't atrophy sickness, isn't claustrophobia, isn't even the food. It's time. It feels longer here. Stretched, distorted somehow. I think it's because there's no horizon.

I grew up on Earth, on the west coast of Ireland in a small, coastal village. At that time, the Atlantic Ocean beyond the coast was full of activity day and night as they constructed ships – interstellar, as opposed to seafaring – on enormous platforms.

But even with all that activity, you could still see the sea and the sky, and knew there was a separation between those two entities. A start and an end, marked always by the passage of the sun.

It's not like that here. Outside, there's only forever. Just that.

The administrator told me Gabriel would be back to me in just two more days. How long is a day up here? I keep forgetting lately.


This is the story Gabriel was in the middle of telling when I first met him, as he and his crew shared a table with me and my team in the crowded station canteen.

There is a planet called Calbrion 7. About seventy years ago a solo pilot named Krystina Bielski went down with her ship. They never found the crash site. It's a big planet, and the jungles there grow fast. No one knew why she was flying in that area, or even why she entered the atmosphere; it's possible her navigation may have malfunctioned. The conclusion was she most likely died in the crash.

Two years after she'd been missing, ships passing by would hear over their audio channels a woman crying. No words, just weeping.

While Gabriel spoke, it seemed like the noise in the whole canteen had been dialled down, and all I could hear was his Catalan-accented voice.

The tale continued. Recently, maybe five years ago, a research group landed to take samples. And they say they saw her there, in the jungle, watching them from amongst the trees.

"Could she have survived? Alone there all that time?" I asked him, drawing his attention to me. His eyes were intense, deep and I felt myself lost in them almost immediately.

He shook his head. "For seventy years? No, she was in her forties when she disappeared. And the atmosphere is poisonous as hell, the air isn't breathable for humans. Something to do with the type of plants growing there. One of the researchers says he saw her without a helmet on. It was just for a few minutes, her watching them, and then she was gone, backed into the jungle and disappeared."

They never did find the crash site.

And I just found the story incredibly sad and excused myself. Gabriel found me later, knocked on my door, apologised needlessly.

"These things happen in space," he said. "It's a price we pay."

"Why?" I asked, eager to talk to him for just a little while longer.

But I also wanted to know.

I stand by the window, looking out into endless everything, backlit by the glow from our quarters. I can hear something clicking behind me, like a dry mouth trying and failing to speak.

Gabriel and I were both born on Earth – very much in the minority these days – but we are very different. I've never felt comfortable up here. It's made my parents proud, done wonders for my career, and I wouldn't have met him otherwise. But still, I often wish I was looking up at the night sky from a small village in Ireland instead of living amongst the stars.

Gabriel isn't like that. He is excited about being in space. He works for a salvage company and has seen far more of the universe than I ever will. Name a known galaxy vector or quadrant or star system within reach of humanity's ships, and Gabriel has done a stint there, or worked with someone who has.

He says he never wants to go back to Earth.

This difference defines us somehow. In my head, he is the universe, but in a tangible body. Something I can touch and know and feel safe with.

He says I am like a beacon. No matter where he is in space, I am how he finds his way home.

I am the fixed centre point to him, while he is eternity to me.

Gabriel is one day away. The administrator visits me again, explaining the situation to me. Gabriel's ship is moving slowly towards us but is now finally within range of the station scans.

She twists her hands as she tells me what those scans are showing. Very little engine propulsion, suggesting emergency reserves. The hull of the ship is damaged, but they can't tell how badly yet.

Communication is down, although that isn't news. It's been that way for two weeks now.

I ask her the question I know she's dreading.

"Life scans are showing three signatures," she says, in a whisper. They don't know who though.

Someone sighs when she says it. I look towards the noise, to a dark corner in the room, but the administrator doesn't seem to notice it.

I thank her and ask her to let me know if any more information becomes available.

Three people are alive on Gabriel's ship.

When he left, there were twelve.

One day. That's all. One more day, whatever that is. I stand in front of the window of our living quarters, staring out, ignoring everything else in the room, all the noises and movement and *presence*, willing myself instead to be a light drawing him close.

We argue a lot about his work.

Gabriel and his crew locate abandoned ships and harvest them for goods and spare parts, sometimes for the companies which own the ships, sometimes not. It's dangerous, but it pays well and there's a lot of work out there.

It's more common than you'd think, ships being abandoned. Engines broke down a lot in the early years of space exploration and when they ran into trouble, crews would wait as long as they could before jettisoning themselves off in escape pods, hoping for a rescue unlikely to arrive.

The empty ships kept floating on regardless, just like any other space debris. There are still tens of thousands ships unaccounted for that we know of, drifting forward silently, like sound itself is trapped inside.

Gabriel makes a living working on ships where most of the crew probably died, and he says my fear is irrational? I say his trust that space is safe is demonstrably foolhardy.

For all his bravado, I find it telling that Gabriel knows so many ghost stories. He needs them, I think. He won't verbalise it, but he's aware of the danger of what he does. Ghost stories cushion him against the fear of this. It makes sense. When our bodies are going into the dangerous unknown, we want to believe that the physical isn't the end of it.

Even in a universe without end.

Especially then.

The earliest ghost story he told me is from the mid-twentieth century, back on Earth.

Launch Complex-34 at Cape Canaveral in Florida was the scene of rocket launches since 1960, but on January 27th, 1967, Astronauts Gus Grissom, Ed White, and Roger Chaffee were burned alive when a fire consumed their Apollo 1 capsule during a launch rehearsal. LC-34 was decommissioned in 1968, and stood alone, the launch platform of four metal and concrete columns rusting and cracking under hot Florida weather.

Employees at Cape Canaveral said they could hear the screams of the astronauts every night around LC-34. There used to be a tour bus which would take visitors to the abandoned launch pad to pay their respects, but this stopped eventually, the tour bypassing the platform entirely.

It's still there in Florida, or parts of it anyway. No one wanted to tear it down.

Finally, I see his ship approach. A speck in the distance that, painfully slowly, draws nearer. The tension in my shoulders, as I watch, feels like a hand resting heavily across them.

I love the stories Gabriel tells me, about a haunted universe where the end isn't the end. I am moved by them, or chilled, or awed, but that is their function.

I love them, but I don't *believe* they're true.

It's natural to wonder what happened to those lost. When someone you love goes out into the unknown, these things weigh on your mind. The contradiction of being faced with an unending universe means that some are desperate that there might be something after that, after infinity.

But if I were to believe the stories are true, then it's also possible to believe he mightn't return.

I can't do that.

I am what guides him back. The light. I won't let that be extinguished. I won't fail him.


The administrator calls at my door. She is to escort me downstairs, asks if I'm ready.

I feel breath behind me, on my neck, urgent and fast. I start to leave and it's like someone is holding my hand, stopping me, trying to drag me backwards but then this grip loosens, and I leave our quarters, refusing to glance behind me as I go.

Why would I look?

There can't be anything there.

I don't feel the surface of the station floor beneath me as I walk: it's as if I'm floating. The station is a hive of activity and life as I pass by, but I hear nothing.

We reach the docking port just as the checks finish, and my senses snap back into place. I feel the floor under my feet, metal bolts against my soles. People are rushing about, yelling abrasively. There is a faint smell of antiseptic and oil.

Someone I don't know is sobbing to my left.

There's a piercing hiss of decompression all around me, and the door to his ship opens.

Robin Maginn is an Irish writer currently living in the UK. He has had several short stories published in print and online, including with *Albedo One, ParAbnormal Digest, Idle Ink,* and *Syntax & Salt.* He was shortlisted for the 2010 Aeon Award (placing third). He was runner up in the Fall 2018 Ghost Story Supernatural Fiction Award and appeared in the anthology *21st Century Ghost Stories: Volume 2.*

# Stitches

## by David Calbert

The blizzard howled like a wounded animal.

Inside the tenuous warmth of the hut, Edda huddled over her work, listening to the wattle frame groan around her. Flecks of clay daub, pressed into walls long ago when her hands had been young, dropped into the low burning fire. The flames spat angry sparks, flickered, and burned on. Edda paused to pull the blanket tighter around her shoulders, the matted tendrils of her grey hair stark against the black moose fur.

If the fire died, Edda would be enfolded with ice before morning. She threw the last of the dry alpine timber into the fire ring, casting her liver-spotted hands in dim shades of orange. She worked slow but steady, kneading the delicate fishbone needle in and out of the shroud. The needle-tip flashed in the firelight, sharp as the edge of the crescent moon. She drew a length of hemp rope up the tanned leather, stitching it closed, a cocoon that would never hatch.

The work would have gone faster if she'd been able to find his remains. A shape to sew around. But she would make do. She would remember Gerben's face as she stitched, and bury the memory in lieu of his body.

A sudden gust of wind yanked the stakes holding the flap over the hut's entrance free, whipping snow and sleet inside. Edda threw herself over the fire, protecting it from the intruding cold. When the flames were healthy enough to bite at her underbelly, Edda got to her feet to close the hut flap.

She halted when she saw the figure in the doorway. Edda made for the spear lying in the corner, determined not to suffer the dishonour of dying unarmed.

Liquid shadows ran from the burgeoning firelight and revealed the figure's face. Gerben's glazed eyes, as brown as tree bark, stared out at her from a mask of snow. His collarbone-length beard and thick eyebrows were nearly solid with ice. His bow and quiver were gone, as was his shirt. But for the tattered pants, his skin was bare.

"Gerben child," she said in disbelief. He came closer, but did not kneel and kiss her hand, giving her a mother's respect. He stepped further into the light, and Edda saw the deep slashes across his torso and arms. The meat inside the wounds had snow-scabbed into hard gems of pain.

"The wolves have had a taste of me," he said. His eyes fell upon the half-stitched shroud. Bending stiffly, Gerben plucked up the needle and handed it to Edda.

"Close me up," he said and smiled. Edda saw blood on his teeth. She took the needle, and they sat beside the fire. This close, she could smell the wild on him, earthy and rank. She looked for creeping black patches that followed exposure to the mould. There were none.

"Thought you were lost to the cold," Edda said.

"I found warmth."

Light danced in his eyes as he watched the needle's slow progress. Edda saw bands of amber bleeding out from Gerben's pupils like sap from an axe-struck tree. She'd known those eyes since he'd been a mewling pink thing swaddled in her arms. They had always been solid brown.

The spear lay a few feet away. With the heel of her foot, Edda rolled it within arm's reach. Gerben didn't seem to notice.

She cinched up the largest slash running up his chest, her needle snagging on the crust of flesh and blood cradled inside. The heat from the fire had melted it some. Pale pink droplets ran over Gerben's chest like ghost blood.

With a quiet crack, the needle broke through the scab, and it sloughed off. Dirty grey fur sprouted from the wound, alive with the scuttling of lice. Edda pulled away with a cry, reaching for the spear at her feet. Gerben's hand snaked out and closed over her arm. A growl rumbled in his chest, resonating inside of him like trapped thunder.

"Mother." The word came out chewed up and spittle-flecked. Not Gerben's voice at all.

Hearing the word mangled so, Edda felt something stir inside of her. The grief that had nestled around her heart for days suddenly caught fire, burning ten times brighter than the coals in the fire ring beside her.

Edda raised the needle and drove it into one of those yellow-brown eyes. She felt something wet and warm run over her fingers. Gerben rolled away, yipping in agony and clawing at his face. Edda grasped the spear and got to her feet. Her old bones groaned, but she got there.

Gerben had come to rest against the far wall of the hut, narrow chest heaving, half his face running with dark blood.

Edda levelled the spear at him.

"End this mockery or lose the other eye."

The body sagged against the wall as if releasing a long-held breath. It shuddered as something inside shifted, turned over and climbed out toward the light.

The grey wolf was long and emaciated, the mangy fur sunken between its sharp ribs, gullies carved by starvation. It crouched in the puddle of Gerben's skin, glaring at Edda with one savage eye.

"Let me stay," the wolf whined, bowing its head beneath Edda's spear. "The forest is hard and cold and delights in filling our bellies only with hunger. I will be a good son."

Edda pressed the spear tip into the wolf's narrow throat.

"Where is Gerben?"

"With the others." The wolf smiled, showing broken, yellow fangs. "I can show you the way. If you promise to let me come home with you."

"You don't belong here," Edda said.

"Please," he whimpered, "I want to live. The pack is culling the weak. They are trying to become... "

His hackles rose and he bit off the end of his sentence. Edda waited, but the wolf would say no more.

Outside the winds picked up and screamed through the cracks in the walls. Edda knew that if her son were still alive, he would not be for long. Her eyes fell onto the grim tapestry of Gerben's skin, which lay beneath the wolf's feet like so much trodden offal.

A guide, even an untrustworthy one, would only increase his chances.

Edda and the wolf ploughed through the snow on the sloping path leading out of the village, heads bowed against the biting wind, growing whiter and whiter until there was no separation between their bodies and the land.

She watched the wolf lope and bob over the icy crust of earth, almost weightless. The blizzard drew Edda's breath from her in long, wispy strips, each one costing her a great effort.

At times the wolf reared up, becoming a grey slash in the storm, before falling back onto its forepaws. Edda thought it was trying to walk on two legs, a trick it was finding hard to do without Gerben's stolen skin.

As they wove up the path and out of the village, they passed the heaped bones of collapsed huts, their clay walls pressed back into the ground from which they were dug. Shadows held up the mouldering doorways as if to invite Edda inside, into the past where the village still thrived.

They cut through the dead fields where long stalks of golden grain and lush vegetation once grew. Several gourds still lay along the edges, soft and rotten. Black mould reached from inside them with long, webbed fingers. Thin veins ran through the mould's glistening surface, and it pulsed, slug-like. The mere sight of it made Edda feel colder than any blizzard ever could.

The wolf paused by a gourd and bent his snout to taste the mouldering rind.

"Don't," Edda warned, and her tone made the wolf's ears lay flat against his skull.

"The climb is long. And I hunger."

"Look around you," Edda said, gesturing back the way they had come. "My village lies in ruin. It's killer festers at your feet. If you taste of that mould, I shall be without a guide."

Confusion and fear filled the animal's amber eyes, but he turned and carried on, leaving the tainted vegetable behind. Edda followed.

It struck her that if she failed to rescue her son, she would be the last of her tribe. There would be no one left to stitch her a shroud. No one to remember her. Her bones cried out in pain, begging her to go inside one of the huts and let the warmth of memory melt the snow off her shoulders. To accept the shadow's black peace. Edda had to pull her feet away from the dead huts, and there was a twinge in the bow of her back, sending a numbness down her legs that had nothing to do with the cold. She closed her eyes and thought of Gerben's face.

The cave entrance opened between the folds of trees like a rocky throat. The wind whistled around its lips, sounding like the long wooden flute Edda used to play before age curled her fingers.

A stack of dead wolves lay off to the side of the entrance, their fur stiff with ice, hard pink tongues jutting from gaping jaws. Some of their lips were black with mould. Black tears stained the cheeks of others. Edda knew that if she were to cut them open, there would be a sticky darkness inside with a hunger greater than any man or animal alive.

The wolf curled his tail up under his legs and sat down.

"I'll go no further," he whined. "They'll kill me like they did the other runts."

Edda peered into the cave. Shadows seemed to gather, waiting to pounce.

Wind whistled in her ears, atonal and lunatic, making her head spin. The day was marked by blood. Edda had lived long enough to know that blood flows according to its own design. The brash fight it, but the wise follow it.

Without a word, she walked past the shivering, one-eyed wolf and descended, come what may.

A fire crackled in the centre of the cavern. The wolves around the flames were the size of Edda's hut, with fur as black and grey as the clouds before a blizzard. A white wolf was on her haunches at the head of the pack, a head-dress of bones rising atop her like colourless thorns. The dress of a shaman. Instead of paws, her front limbs ended in hairless pink appendages. Things that looked like human hands. Almost.

Edda looked past the wolves and saw her son, lying on a bed of leaves. His exposed meat shone slickly in the firelight, oozing blood like a sponge full to burst with water. A cloud of flies hovered just above him but never lighting upon the deep red gore, as if held back by some invisible sheet. Gerben's eyes bulged with conscious agony. Brown, without a trace of amber.

Clay bowls laid in a line by his side, collecting the flow as it ran off him.

"Mother," the Shaman-wolf said. She stood up on her back paws, and her pointed ears brushed against the roof of the chamber. The bones on her head seemed to speak without words, like teeth clicking together.

"I've come for him."

"We need the knowledge in his blood, Mother-Edda."

"Why?"

The Shaman-wolf spread her pink hands. Edda saw lines forming on the palms. Life lines. Love lines. Fate lines.

"To become like you. To survive."

"We fare no better against this pestilence," Edda said.

A worried whine tittered among the pack. They turned to the Shaman-wolf.

"We will be stronger," the Shaman-wolf said.

"Becoming like us won't protect you from what's killing the land. Let him go."

The Shaman-wolf's pink tongue lolled out, running over her snout as she considered.

"My magic is the only thing keeping him alive," she said. "He will die outside the cave."

"Survival is more than a beating heart," Edda said., "It is memory. If you had truly become like us, you would know that."

Edda reached into the folds of her cloak and brought out a strip of something matted. Holding it in the firelight, the wolves saw that it was a torn swatch of runt pelt, stiff with cold. Edda was careful not to touch the frozen meat inside when she turned it over to show them the mould. Amber eyes glared down at her, wide and glowing. And Edda knew that simply seeing was not enough.

She pressed one gnarled index finger into the pulsing mould. Threads of the black substance wove up her skin, pulling hungrily at the fresh meat. Burning pain ran up her arm, but she refused to let it show. Nothing must distract from what she was showing them.

The wolves watched as the mould flayed the pad of her finger and slithered inside.

"We are the last of our village." Edda dropped her decaying finger and cast a long, heavy glance at her son.

"Soon, we will be gone. Please, let me take my son home."

The Shaman-wolf lowered her head, lips pulling back from long, sharp teeth. Her fingers curled into fists. Another wolf came forward, her muzzle frosted with the grey of old age. Edda saw hairless patches of scar tissue stretching across her flank. The other wolves shrank back, bowing their heads.

"Give him back," she said, the authority in her voice quiet but unmistakable. The Shaman-wolf growled a challenge, the bones of her head-dress vibrating with power.

"We need him."

The Scarred wolf lashed out. Her paws, which were still those of a wolf, slashed at the headdress. The bones clattered across the stone floor, trembled once, and lay still. With a terrified yelp, the Shaman-wolf lowered her white body to the floor, pink palms turned up in prostration.

"Your magic has failed." The Scarred wolf said. "We must find another way."

She turned to Edda, who saw that the old wolf's eyes were not amber, but brown.

"Take him and go."

The others parted, making a path to her son.


The one-eyed wolf was waiting when Edda and Gerben emerged. As they passed, he fell into step beside them, head bowed as if in mourning.


Gerben made it to the edge of the forest. The tendons in his feet slid between the straining muscles, leaving a trail of pink snow behind. Edda saw several small animals dart from behind trees to nibble the leavings; rodents, birds, and one scrawny fox with half an ear chewed off. Black mould clung to its face. The one-eyed wolf's gait never wavered, nor did his pink tongue dart out for a taste.

Despite the wind and snow, Gerben only shivered once, right at the end. Before he died, he kissed Edda's hand and whispered something in her ear. She tried hard to hear, but she had the ears of an old woman, and the wind was jealously loud. As she stood, she saw the wolf's ears raised and alert. He averted his eyes and sat hunched in the snow, waiting.

Edda tied one of her furs around Gerben's ankles, cinching them tight. When she held out one end to the wolf, he took it in his mouth without complaint. Together, they dragged him the rest of the way. She thought the effort might kill her too, but it seemed that the blood-marked day was sated.

Edda found the fishbone needle where she'd left it, lying in a pool of wolf blood near the fire. After cleaning it off, she fetched the crumpled skin and smoothed out the creases. First the skin, she thought, and then the shroud. Without the use of her ruined finger, the needle felt awkward in her hand.

The one-eyed wolf sat just outside the hut, watching her, not daring to come in. After the third miss at threading the needle, Edda bade the wolf come in. He did, shaking snow off his fur.

"Hold it in place," Edda said, indicating the next spot of her threadwork.

"Let me wear it."

"No," Edda said firmly.

"Why?"

"Because we respect the dead. And we do not try to live as someone we're not. Now help me."

The wolf placed a paw against the skin.

As Edda used her good hand to finish the stitching, she noted that while the wolf had nothing like the shaman's human hands, his fingers seemed longer than usual. More dexterous.

Gerben's body filled the skin, giving it shape. When his face settled upon the bones of his cheeks and jaw, he seemed momentarily alive. Edda's grief broke then, and she wept through the rest of her work.

A sudden warmth pressed against her hand. Edda looked down and saw the wolf's chin nuzzling. Comforting.

"Do you have a name?" Edda asked. The wolf paused, as if afraid to answer.

"They call me Gnasher," he said finally.

"Help me with the shroud, Gnash." Edda noted a faint shine in his eye at the informal use of his name, but he said nothing.

It was faster, stitching the shroud the second time. Together, the wolf and Edda buried the flesh and skin within the shroud. Edda walked back from the grave – with the wolf close behind, hands empty for the first time all day. But they would never be truly empty. She kept the memory of her son close to her like an ember burning on a cold night.

Exhaustion wracked Edda's body and she lay down to rest. The fire had faded to embers. Grabbing a stick, Edda prodded it back to life. As she did, she saw the long black threads weaving up her arm.

The storm outside was waning, and quiet worked its way into the hut like a poisonous cloud. Gnasher lay on the other side of the fire, watching the light dance. He yawned, jaws wide enough for Edda to stick her head in, his pink tongue rolling over his jagged teeth. At the pinnacle of the yawn, Edda saw the place where mouth became throat. Black fingers crawled up from his depths.

"Tell me a story, Gnash."

"What is a story?"

Edda smiled softly, watching the flames.

"How we remember. How we stay human."

"Show me."

Edda did.

And outside, the storm gave one final howl before disappearing into silence.

David Calbert's fiction has been published in *The Berekely Fiction Review, Theme of Absence, Tales from the Moonlit Path,* and *Horrified Magazine.* He lives in Portland Oregon.

# Licked Clean

by Jen Cornick

"It looks more like a sugar pull for ribbon candy," Holly said, looking at the blob of marmalade that was supposed to be wobbly. She poked at the still-warm jam with the end of a wooden spoon. It barely moved. "I ruined your Christmas gift," she said to Colan, her eyebrows knitting together as she looked up at him. "And your pot."

"You tried, *elskan mín*," he said, biting his cheek to hide a laugh. "You've never been able to make jam."

"But everybody makes jam."

"You are a brilliant professor of literature. You don't need to make jam."

"I should have learned how to by now." She'd been trying to make jam since last winter, when she'd moved to Iceland. And had still not succeeded. Every time it was burnt, or under done, or wouldn't set, or the lids wouldn't pop. It wasn't just unsuccessful. Every time was a relative disaster.

"At least it didn't explode this time," he said, wrapping his arm around her shoulders and squeezing her to his side. And that made her feel just a little bit better. Until he laughed.

"It really isn't funny," she said, putting the lid back on the pot and pushing it to the back of the stove. It scraped against the old electrical elements, making Holly wince and squeeze her eyes shut. "I hate that noise."

"We should clean that," he said, kissing her temple to erase the sting of his laughter.

"Later," she said, picking at the cooling sugar at the end of the wooden spoon.

"Ah, but we really should. 'Tis the season after all,", his voice deepened

and softened as though he were preparing to tell a story. She loved it when he sounded like that. In fact, that was how they met, she had drifted into his lecture hall, listening to him tell the tale of the witch and the stone boat to a class of students all leaning forward at their desks.

"Christmas," she said darkly, pointing at the jars that had already been labelled for him.

"The benign part of the season, gift-giving. The tree. The *jolabokaflod*."

She turned into his chest then, leaning her forehead against his shoulder. "I'm looking forward to my first Yule book flood actually, so don't take that away from me," Holly said, poking him through his thick wool sweater, right in the centre of one of the diamonds that radiated out from the frayed collar.

"But then there's the rest," he said, his tone deepening. A low rumble that she felt right through her. "*Gryla* the Witch who snatches misbehaving children for her stew pot. She has fifteen tails and carries a bag and a sword; skewering every rotten child she sees."

"Almost as bad as the Austrians then," she said, settling against him as his arms tightened around her.

"She is much worse than Krampus," he said with a light chuckle. "He's tempered by St Nicholas. She is not."

"The witch doesn't explain why I have to clean that pot," she said, her tone slightly petulant.

"Other than we'll not have a pot to make hot chocolate or spiced wine or mulled cider tomorrow?" She could hear the smile in his voice, and that made her smile in return.

"Other than that, yes. A better reason for us not to run to the store this instant and buy a new pot."

"Well, the dirty pot would still be here and that'll draw the Yule Lads."

"They sound benign."

"As benign at Christmas as their mother," he said with a deep chuckle. "They plague houses in the thirteen days before Christmas, stealing sausages, licking spoons, slamming doors. *Gryla* sets her sons loose in the town when it's quietest. And then she screams and howls, collecting them all to her again."

"Still doesn't explain why I must wash the pot, my dear folklorist."

"Because one of them is called Pot-Licker," he said, just as his phone pinged on the table.

"Saves me cleaning the pot then," she said, patting his chest just before leaving his arms.

"Where her sons are, *Gryla* follows." Colan picked up his phone from the table and quickly scrolled through it. "You'll be here when I get back?" he asked before giving her a quick peck on the cheek.

She nodded, running water in the kitchen sink. Ostensibly, she still had an apartment near the university, but most of her things were here. Her dressing-gown was draped over the bench that sat at the end of his bed upstairs. And her books and notebooks were scattered all over. In fact, all that was left at the apartment she still paid rent on for no reason, was books.

"It's Jon, so I might be late." His keys jangled as he shrugged on his parka near the front door. "Wash the pot," he said with a wink.

She drifted away from the sink and stood in the kitchen door, watching him. "Buy a new pot, since you're leaving me all alone in your house."

"Hardly just my house now," he said with a chuckle as he closed the door behind him. Which meant he missed her blush completely.

She let herself smile as she straightened cushions on the couch and collected their unread books from the various places they usually forgot about them, pointedly ignoring the pot of semi-hard-orange-candy-that-should-have-been-marmalade on the back of the stove. It was an hour and a half before the text came in, saying that things were taking longer, that he would be later than he thought. So, she ate dinner without him, staring at the pot of sugar. And then she climbed the stairs, leaving the pot on the back of the stove on purpose, while she pulled on her pyjamas and read in bed.


It was the persistent, rattling, shaking sound that woke her. The one that made her wince and her eyes shut tighter, even when half asleep.

"Colan?" she called, feeling the cold sheets next to her as the that spine-scratching metallic shuffle continued. "Come to bed, we'll deal with the pot in the morning." It was more than slightly grumpy sounding, she knew. But he just wouldn't stop shaking the pot on the stove.

The wind screamed past the windows, sounding like a nightmare train from a slasher-film version of *Thomas the Tank Engine*. It made her shiver, reaching for her dressing-gown on the bench at the end of the bed. She shoved her feet into cold slippers.

"Colan," she called out flicking the lights on in the upstairs hallway and looking over the railing to the ground floor. There was no answer except for the pot shaking. And this time it made her wince and flinch. She stood still for a moment, hoping that it was all her imagination. That she wasn't hearing things in the deepest, darkest parts of the night.

The pot rattled again, that grating shuffling shake of metal.

She jumped and braced herself against the wall. "What is that?" She could hear the tremor in her own voice as she started to creep down the stairs.

Holly peeked into the kitchen. The pot rattled, the lid shaking as it shuffled on the burner. She couldn't see it but she could hear it.

It could be a rat.

That made her gag. She couldn't remember if Iceland had rats, as she reached for something heavy enough to bat whatever was in the pot away once she lifted the lid.

It could be a bat.

But that was almost as bad as a rat. That made her gag again, acidic and awful. She looked at the dripping wooden spoon she had pulled from the sink, sticky with dissolved sugar. Unlikely to protect against rabies. But it was the best she could do.

The pot shook, moving closer to the edge of the stove as Holly took a step forward. She held the spoon out in front of her, like a fencer holds a sword. The lid popped up and then rattled on the rim as she lunged forward and poked the pot with the spoon. It slid back an inch, if she was being generous, and then rattled forward again.

"What the hell is this?" she asked, poking it.

The lid popped up and then slammed down again, but not before Holly caught sight of two large, almost human looking eyes reflecting what little light there was.

"Heaving handfuls of hell," she whispered, her heart not entirely sure which beat was needed, that slow counting waltz of relief or the panic pounding one of fear.

The wooden spoon clattered to the floor. But it still didn't stop the pot from rattling and shuffling on the stove. In fact, it seemed to pointedly ignore her. Wet, slurping sounds came from inside. It was wholly occupied by burnt orange peel and hardened sugar. Which was fortunate, given that her impulse was to slam her hands down on the lid and hold it closed.

So, she did.

As she held the lid down, whatever was in there started to bang against the sides and keen – that whine a new hellscape of sound – surreal and echoing. It nearly made her let go of the lid. The thing inside pushed up with some force, almost dislodging one of her hands.

She leaned on the pot, dragging it across the stove to the counter   top. Keeping her weight on the lid, she opened the drawer and started digging, looking for the twine she made Colan buy so they could tie herbs together when they made soup. In this pot.

Winding the twine around the lid and handles, she tied it shut as best she could.

As she backed away from the pot, she slapped her hand against the light switch and blinked against the sudden wash of light. The thing inside the pot screamed. It sounded like the steam from a thousand discordant kettles. The pot bounced to the floor and whatever was inside it groaned.

Holly slid to the ground against the wall, watching the pot roll across the floor. A laugh spilled from her before she could stop it, frenzied and sharp-edged. It didn't sound like her at all. She'd never laughed like this. But she couldn't stop. It was always like this, when her emotions were this extreme, crying when she should have been shouting in anger and laughing when anyone else would have been screaming.

Her sides ached with it. Her lungs burned with each new giggling exhale as panic and relief collided. It felt odd; her heart stopping and re-starting all at once.

"Police won't believe me," she said, through a fit of hyperventilating breaths. "No point in phoning them." She collapsed to laughter once again. She almost felt drunk. Light-headed and topsy-turvy.

"Simon's a biologist. He'll know," she said, lurching forward onto her hands and knees, she snagged the twine and pulled the pot with her when she crawled from the kitchen. Pressing her brother's contact information, calling him in Qatar.

"Holly, it is two in the morning." Simon's voice was still slurred with sleep when he picked up his cell phone.

"I caught something," she said, a fit of giggles followed.

"You have a fever?" he asked, suddenly seeming more alert. "How high is it? Do you need to go to the hospital? Does Colan know? Is he there?"

"No, he's out, and it's in the marmalade pot. Trapped," she said, knowing she sounded odd. Knowing her brother would be worried but she couldn't move past it, get around it, and it just made her laugh harder.

"I'm calling Colan."

"How is an Icelandic folklorist going to help me get rid of a haunted rat-bat hybrid with human eyes?" Each word was punctuated by a giggle or a rasping gasp for air.

"A what? Feverish hallucinations." She wasn't meant to hear that part. Simon then spent several minutes trying to talk Holly into taking deep breaths, but she was unable to do anything other than curl up and giggle on the floor as the pot wandered around her, rattling and raging.

She heard, but could not register, Colan's familiar step in the hall. "Holly," his voice cut through her laughter, the thing's screaming, the chattering of the phone on the floor and the clanging of the pot. He propped her up against the wall and picked up her phone. "Just a bit panicked. She wouldn't have called unless she thought it was an emergency."

Setting the phone on the table, he crouched down. "Let's see what you've caught," he said, taking the twine from her hands and wound it around his fingers.

"You'll see," she sang.

He untied the lid, holding it tight to the pot as it rattled and raged. "*Fjandans*," Colan whispered as he peeked inside.

A flood of haunting, squeaking, whining, screeching Icelandic curses poured forth from the pot. Holly's sharp-edged, feverish laughter finally stopped.

"I didn't think they were real," Colan said with more than a little wonder, and far too much reverence for the haunted rat or possessed bat that had learned to speak while she was on the phone. He whipped the lid of the pot and at the same time pulled something wriggling out of it.

The squirming thing was wearing doll shoes on its feet and a rough-spun wool coat. And it just cursed louder. "Holly, meet *Pottasleiki*, or Pot-Licker. One of the Yule Lads." Colan held the little punching gnome by his long white beard.

"Pleased to meet you."

Pot-Licker, covered in shards of orange peel and straggling strands of sugar twisted around in Colan's hands to look at Holly. And promptly, kicked at her nose with his plastic high-heeled shoe.

Colan chuckled. "He's a feisty one. Living up to his reputation, I suppose. But if he's here, his mother will be somewhere around."

The wind screamed past the windows, rattling them in their frames. That haunted, hellish wailing of a train whistle resounded through the house. It crawled over her skin and made it pebble with goose pimples, even though the temperature hadn't changed.

"There she is. *Gryla*," Colan said, far calmer than he should be given that demonic screech.

"She sounds like a treat," Holly said, pushing up from the floor.

"I told you she was unpleasant," he said, grabbing her elbow as she stood, helping her steady herself.

"And I thought it was just a story."

"So did I. Let's just put him back outside for his mother to collect," Colan said, opening the front door. "He's not worth *Gryla*'s wrath." He put the little, violent, sugar-covered gnome on the front step and slammed the door. "Now, let's clean this pot. Heaven only knows who else was about tonight. We'll need to check our spoons."

# Soliloquy of an Inverted Solipsist

by Taliesin Gore

Since no one passed me on my walk today
It all appears to me as in a dream.
I, as I make my unreported way
Through barren, sodden, sullen fields, now seem
An ambulating phantom on a path
Through hinterlands that only half exist,
A half-limned figure in a photograph
Framed, never taken – fading in the mist
Where all things cease to be that are not seen.
I wonder: if all my life passed unobserved
By others' eyes, would I have really been
Here at all? Or would I be *un-birthed*
Out of the world into the under-void?
Please tell me I'm just being paranoid.

Taliesin Gore's poetry and fiction have appeared or are upcoming in various places, including *Bleed Error, The Metaworker, MetaStellar,* and on YouTube at HorrorBabble. He has been a two-time Finalist in Omnidawn's Fabulist Fiction Contest, and his poem "Unnatural Theology" won an Honourable Mention in the Wergle Flomp Humour Poetry Contest 2023. He lives in an annexe in his mother's garden.

# Contact the BFS

The British Fantasy Society is run by many people, all unpaid, in their spare time. Here's a list of the email addresses for those currently involved. If you would like to contribute to the BFS in any way, then please feel free to email the appropriate person. If you would like to volunteer for a post, contact the chair.

## COMMITTEE

**President Elect** — Juliet Mushens
president@britishfantasysociety.org
**Chair** — Shona Kinsella
chair@britishfantasysociety.org
**Membership Secretary** — Karen Fishwick
secretary@britishfantasysociety.org
**Treasurer** — John Dodd
treasurer@britishfantasysociety.org
**BFS Horizons Editor** — Pete Sutton
bfshorizons@britishfantasysociety.org
**BFS Journal Editor** — Sean Wilcock
bfsjournal@britishfantasysociety.org
**Web Administrator** — John Stabler (technical matters only, not content)
webmaster@britishfantasysociety.org
**Events Coordinator** — [vacant]
events@britishfantasysociety.org
**British Fantasy Awards Administrator** — Katherine Fowler
bfsawards@britishfantasysociety.org
**Communications Officer** — Jenn Arndt
communications@britishfantasysociety.org

**Stockholder** — [vacant]

stockholder@britishfantasysociety.org

**Online Content Editor** — Jessica Triana de Ford

online@britishfantasysociety.org

**Reviews Editor** — Sarah Deeming

bookreviews@britishfantasysociety.org

**BFS Horizons Poetry Editor** — Ian Hunter

poetry@britishfantasysociety.org

**Short Story Competition** — Steven Poore

shortstorycomp@britishfantasysociety.org


## EVENT CONTACTS

**London Events Organiser** — Karen Fishwick

events@britishfantasysociety.org

**Sheffield Events Organiser (in partnership with the BSFA) —** Steve Poore

steven.poore@hotmail.com

**York Events Organiser (in partnership with the BSFA) —** Alex Bardy

mangozine@btinternet.com

**Glasgow Events Organiser** — Shona Kinsella

shona.kinsella@outlook.com


**www.britishfantasysociety.org**